CRAVED

A DEVILS BLAZE MC NOVELLA

JORDAN MARIE

CRAVED

A Devil's Blaze MC Novella
By: Jordan Marie

Annie

Some men defy description.

I deal with books. I know every adjective in the English language and I can't describe Sabre.

He's a biker with a filthy mouth and a dirty mind and he sets me on fire.

I've lived in the shadows my whole life, afraid to see what is beyond my own little corner of the world.

Sabre makes me step outside my safe zone.

He makes me **crave**...more.

Sabre

Annie is everything I shouldn't want.

From that uptight dress to the hair she wears in a damn bun, down to those black rimmed glasses. We don't fit. A librarian and a biker, and if that's not cliché enough, she has cats!

I should run.

I'm not going to. One taste and I only want more.

There's a tiger hiding behind that uptight prude disguise she's wearing and once I get my teeth into her...

I'm never letting go.

1

SABRE

I t's happened to my brothers before—so, I know it can. That thunderbolt feeling that strikes you with just one look. I just never fucking expected it to happen to me. I'm the most jaded motherfucker to walk the face of the Earth. There's a reason I wound up a member of the Devil's Blaze Motorcycle Club. I don't fucking deal well with rules, I don't deal well with people, and I don't like living life the way some other fucker tells me I should. So, the fact that I'm standing here in the middle of a fucking street in the small, sleepy town of Slade, Kentucky, panting after some uptight bitch, knocks me on my ass.

It's August for fuck's sake and one of the hottest months ever on record. It's easily a hundred and two out here and this bitch is wearing a long-sleeved, gray dress that comes up to her damn chin and some kind of fancy nylon tights on her legs under that. About the only thing that looks like she dressed for the weather is the tight little bun she's pulled her white-gold hair into and, fuck me, that looks *painful*. The thing is, despite how stupid the outfit is, it *is* sexy as hell. The dress hugs curves that go on for fucking miles. Tits that would more than fill my hands, and legs... fuck, those legs were made to wrap around a man. Hell, those pointy-heeled shoes she has on, alone, make my dick stand up and take notice.

I want to pull that hair down and wrap it around my hand while I'm feeding her every inch of my cock. Her skin is creamy milk with just a hint of color, and she has these thick-rimmed, black glasses on and everything about her screams uptight teacher. Hell, suddenly I want to go back to school. She's looking under the hood of a beat-up, old Chevy Blazer and waving steam out of her face. I can already tell its overheating. Then again, *so am I.*

"Car trouble?" I ask, sounding bored, but honestly I'm anything but. Shit, if my cock gets any harder, I'm going to have to jack off right here in the middle of the street.

She looks up at me and even through the glasses I can see the prettiest blue eyes I've ever laid sight on. *Damn. It just keeps getting better.* Her sweet, little pink tongue comes out and brushes across her lips, and any brain cells I had left that weren't already directing energy to my dick are gone now.

"Uh...yes...I called Triple A, though," she says and her voice is sweet and soft, and I'm dying to know how it sounds when full of pleasure.

"You're not from around here are you, honey?"

"I...I just moved here from Illinois. I took the job at the county library."

Librarian. Fuck me, my brain keeps telling me to turn away, and if I could talk any sense at all into my dick right now, I would. That ship has sailed, though. I'm going to nail this woman, it's just a matter of *when* at this point.

"I thought so," I mumble, looking under the hood of her vehicle. I'm pretty sure I know the problem, but just to make sure, I get down on the ground and crawl under the SUV.

"You don't have to do this. I'm sure they'll be sending someone out any minute now."

"That's why I knew you weren't from around here. You're in

the backwoods of Kentucky, honey. Nearest tow would be Ray's, two counties over, and when he gets here, he'll either be shit-faced, horny, or both."

"I...I'm sure...I can find someone..."

"Your water pump is blown," I inform her, deciding to lay on the ground a moment longer because the view of those fucking fantastic legs of hers that I'm getting through the slit of her skirt is amazing. *Jesus.*

"I...will that take a long time to fix?" She asks, looking down at her...*Mickey Mouse watch?*

I get up and slam the hood down on her ride and watch as she steps back to look at me. Those blue eyes of hers are wide, but I'm not sure if it's with fear or something else. Her nipples are hard and poking through that tight-ass dress, so I'm hoping it's some-thing else entirely.

"What's your name, honey?"

"Um...Annabelle."

"Of course it is," I answer, shaking my damn head. Hell, even her name is wholesome.

"I'm sorry?" She asks, those blue eyes full of confusion.

"Not a thing, Annie, not a damn thing. Okay, let's load you on my bike and get you home. I'll get one of the boys to fix your car and drop it off."

"You...I mean, do you run a garage?"

"Something like that," I agree, shaking my head.

I follow as she goes around to the driver's side of her car and gets her purse and some folders. She bends over and that clingy fabric she's wearing tightens up on her ass, and I nearly cum in my fucking jeans. As it is, I can't stop the groan that leaves my lips. She straightens up and looks back at me. Her gaze goes down and watches my hand. The hand just happens to be palming my cock so I can adjust myself. Heat rises on her cheeks and it looks fucking good on her. I don't think I've ever known a woman who blushes.

"I'm not sure I should be going anywhere with you...Mr....
What was your name again?"

"Sabre."

"*Sabre?*"

"That's my name, honey. Now, it's hotter than hell out here
and I'm looking for you to stroke out any minute, so how about
you get a move on and haul your ass to my bike."

"Your bike?"

"Yeah, my bike."

"I'm not dressed to ride on a bike, Mr....umm...Sabre."

She's fucking sweet. So sweet she makes me want to taste her
to see if her pussy is as sweet as she is. I bet she's luscious and
juicy like a peach.

"Honey, get your shit. I got things to do, and I'm not leaving
you out in this heat." When she continues not to move and just
stares at me, I sigh heavily. "Do it Annie, or I'll carry you. It's your
choice."

She jerks at my words. Then she continues watching me for a
minute. Finally, she must have assumed *(correctly)* that I wasn't
kidding and starts walking away. I grab her arm just to make sure
she doesn't get away and lead her to my bike. The muscles in her
wrist tighten up under my hold, but she doesn't pull away. It takes
her three tries to get on the back of my bike with that long-ass
skirt and fuck-me shoes. I watch it all over my shoulder and love
the way the dress pulls up to her knees. I grieve that I'm on a
deadline because I'd love to get a look at what she's hiding under
that dress. I will, eventually. I make myself that promise.

"Where do you live, honey?"

"The old farmhouse on Turkey Ridge?"

A farmhouse? I'm still shaking my head as I pull out on the
street. Ms. Annie has hit me like a motherfucking thunderbolt.
I'm screwed.

2

ANNIE

WHEN YOUR FATHER IS A MINISTER, YOU CAN GO WILD OR
STAY SAFE. WHEN YOUR FATHER IS ALSO A MONSTER, YOU
PICK SAFE. STILL, I'VE ALWAYS WONDERED WHAT LIFE WAS
LIKE ON THE WILD SIDE.

E very warning my father ever drummed in my head is replaying. Every beating I ever took by his belt flashes in my memory. You might think those memories would disappear since I am now twenty-six years old. They don't. They are always there...heavy in my chest and lying like a weight holding me down. Still, when this big *(and I mean huge)* man stands in front of me wearing faded jeans, a white t-shirt, a black leather vest, dirty-blond hair, sunglasses, and tattoos...*everywhere*...my first instinct *isn't* to run. No, my first instinct is to lick him from head to toe. I obviously don't, but the more he looks at me like he wants to eat me up, the more I'm tempted. I briefly think of my favorite bedtime story as a kid, *'Little Red Riding Hood'*. No wonder Little Red ended up being eaten by the wolf. If the wolf were anywhere near as potent as the man in front of me, I would have, too.

Temptation. That's it, really. He is a temptation, and I really should walk away. How many times has it been drummed into my head that temptation comes before the fall? This man has danger written all over him. There's no way I could survive any type of a fall if he's involved. *He's not safe. He's not for me.* That's the mantra I keep replaying in my mind as he drives me home. I try to ignore the scent of him I catch on the wind, or how my arms feel wrapped around him. *I try*. I'm not sure I succeed.

When we pull into my faded, blacktop driveway, I breathe a sigh of relief that this is over. Now, I can steer away from him and ignore the feeling of sadness that gives me. It takes me two tries to get off his bike, I guess that's an improvement from getting on. I hold my hand on Sabre's shoulder to steady myself. I almost fall trying to stand on the small point of my six- inch heels. Sabre's large, muscular hand grabs my hip and steadies me. I stare at him and wish his sunglasses were gone.

"Careful there, Annie," his husky voice tells me and chills of awareness slide up my spine. There's a heat where his hand covers my hip. It warms in intensity and spreads slowly over my body. It's more than just electricity. Can he feel it, too? His fingers flex and again, I grieve the fact I can't see his eyes. He took off his sunglasses when he crawled under my car, but I didn't get to see their color. *I really want to.*

"Thank you for your help," I tell him, closing my right hand into a fist and letting my fingernails dig into the palm of my hand. I use that small bite of pain to help me concentrate because all I really want to do is touch him.

"I'll have the boys drop off your ride tonight."

"Are you sure? It's late? I don't want to cause…"

"I'm sure. I have an errand to do for the club, but I'll check back."

Okay, so I can admit to myself that I was kind of hoping he would at least *try* to come inside. It's crazy but true all the same. I give him a small smile.

"If you have them bring a bill, I'll pay them. Thank you again, Sabre."

"Be seeing you soon."

I walk away and don't respond to his words.

"Annie?" Sabre yells, just as I make it to my front door.

I turn to look at him, pasting on the smile I give all the customers at the library where I work. "Yes?"

"I said I'll be seeing you," he claims again, his voice frank but full of promise.

"I doubt that," I answer honestly.

"Why's that?"

"You don't look like the kind of guy to come in a library. I doubt you've ever been in one."

His bark of laughter follows me into the house.

3

SABRE

A SMART MAN WOULD RUN FROM TROUBLE UNLESS THAT
TROUBLE HAS A BODY THAT DOESN'T QUIT. THEN HE GRABS
IT AND RIDES THE FUCK OUT OF IT.

I watch her ass sway as she walks inside, hypnotized by the movement. I'm still laughing. *You don't look like the kind of guy to come in a library.* Little girl has no idea. I'm going to come. I'm going to come a lot in that damn library. I'm going to come so often that every minute she's at work she'll not be able to concentrate. All she will do is remember all the places where I fucked her unconscious and left her full of my cum.

I don't even like denying myself now, but I do. Skull sent me on a job today, and I got to get that shit finished. We've been having some trouble with a rival club that followed us here out of Georgia. The Chrome Saints were ruled over by Visor, an old son of a bitch that was evil through and through. The world would be a better place if he no longer drew breath. He hated Skull. I'm not sure what the beef was between the two, but I know that it had something to do with Skull's old lady, Beth. All any of us really knows is that Visor and Skull have a personal war that spewed over into the clubs. There was a war, but after we had lost Beth, a tentative truce was put in place. The last year has been quiet and a welcome relief after all of the uproar in the past.

Losing Beth has been hard on Skull, and we enjoy the quiet

we have found here. At least we had until yesterday, when reports filtered in that another MC Club was spotted close to our territory. At first we didn't think much about it. We figured it was Dragon and the boys, but after getting a detailed description on their jackets, it was best we check it out. One of the reasons Skull makes such a good fucking President is that we never get caught with our pants down. I'm not about to let that change now, just because I have a hard-on for a piece of tail. The club comes first.

Always.

"WHAT THE HELL do you mean there was no sign, hermano?"

"Exactly what I said, Boss. There was no sign of any club in the area. Locals denied it, our police contacts denied it, and hell, we even searched hotels in the area looking for bikes. It was a wild goose chase."

"Something is going on, or we would not have heard the rumors," Skull responds, and while I agree with him, I am at a loss on what our next move is. Pistol, the club VP, is not quite as impassive.

"I think it's time we take over the Savage Clubhouse. I haven't trusted that fucker, Dragon, from day one. I know you have this deal with him, but that asshole is shady."

It's an old fight. Skull has gotten pretty close with the Savage Crew. Pistol and Briar were against entering into an alliance with them; however, majority still ruled and most of the club only saw us being stronger with the Savage Brothers on our side. I voted to go ahead with the alliance myself. I hadn't seen anything I disliked from the other club.

"Ciérralo!" Skull orders and the room goes quiet. It is an old fight between the Pres and his second, and it's easy to tell that the Pres is getting tired of the shit storm that Pistol keeps making out of it. "It is done. Majority vote made the decision and that is final. El fin. Si?"

Pistol stares hard at Skull but, eventually, backs down. You can feel the tension in the room, though. It's thick. The saying *'you could cut it with a knife'* comes to mind. Those two are going to go head to head soon and if Pistol gains control of the club, I won't stay. I'll go back to the main chapter in Georgia. He's a hot head, and I'm not about to lay my ass on the line, daily, for him. My loyalty is to Skull. He's saved our asses time and time again. If Pistol gets the club, there's no way it will remain the same.

"Where are Beast and Torch?" I ask because it's way too fucking quiet in the main clubhouse.

"They are at that woman's house you sent Keys and Shaft to," Briar answers before anyone else, and I'm instantly annoyed.

"What the fuck are Torch and Beast doing there? I sent the prospects to fix the water pump and deliver her truck. Where are they?"

"Still there. When Torch called to check and see what the hold-up was, Keys told him the hot little mama was fixing them dinner as a thank you. So he and Beast decided to go check her out."

"Fuck me!" I growl getting up.

"What is wrong, hermano?" Skull asks, but I hear the laughter in his voice. The motherfucker already knows why I'm upset.

"I'm going to go drag the dogs away from my woman."

"You best hurry, you know how the coño flock to the Beast man. They all want a piece of his gran polla."

I walk off on that, giving them my back as the laughter erupts around me. I flip them off going out the door. It only makes them laugh harder.

If Annie is giving those fuckers anything, I'll turn her ass bright red.

4

ANNIE

CURIOSITY KILLED THE CAT, I'M NOT QUITE SURE WHAT IT'S
GOING TO DO TO ME.

O nce Sabre dropped me off, I was at loose ends. I endured an hour long conversation with my mother, hearing again the one hundred reasons I should be living back home. After that, I was so stressed that I decided to do what I always do, get lost in the kitchen. I go into the bedroom and grab my favorite gray yoga pants, put on my sports bra and a pink, (almost faded white) t-shirt over top of that. Feeling much more relaxed and at ease, I undo the chignon I had my hair in and just gather it into a ponytail on the top of my head. My hair is long, so even pulled up like that, the bottom of the ponytail still comes to the middle of my back.

Once all that is done, I go into the kitchen, grab all the fixings for my meatloaf and begin making dinner. I love to cook. It is part of the reason my ass refuses to fit in anything but a size fourteen these days. I don't mind; I actually like the size I am. I'm comfortable with my body and my life. There's not much I would change, except maybe my parents and the scars from my childhood. Those would be nice to live without.

The timer for the meatloaf is just going off when the doorbell rings. I pull it out of the oven, leaving it on the stove top and hurry to the door. Looking through the peephole I see two men. The one in front is tall and muscular. He's got on a black t-shirt, but his arms and hands are covered in ink, he has on sunglasses, and his dark hair reminds me of a warm cup of coffee. Behind him stands another man, less tattoos, and with blond, sandy hair. He doesn't have as much ink and he's definitely skinnier, but you can tell he's in good shape. He's got friendly green eyes, and he's wearing this smile that for some reason makes me want to smile, too. I get a little nervous wondering why they are at my door and shake it off a moment later. My parents have managed to make me afraid of my shadow. These guys are probably just from Sabre's garage. I open the door, leaving the chain latched and look at the two men.

"Can I help you?"

"Sabre asked us to fix your car and drop it off," the guy in the front says.

I smile and relax a little more. "Just a second," I tell him, closing the door. I undo the latch on the chain and open it all the way. The man hands me the keys to my Blazer. "How much do I owe you?" The guy looks startled when I ask. The other man that was behind him comes around to stand beside him now. They both look at me grinning like they know a secret I don't. It's very unnerving.

"I'm sure Sabre will give you a bill," the smaller of the two says with an easy laugh.

I frown because I specifically told him to have his mechanics bring me the bill. Still, it's not their fault, and I feel bad that they've had to work so hard in this heat.

"Thank you so much for getting it done so quickly. Would you like something to drink? I mean it's so hot outside, and I feel terrible that you've been out in it for me."

"I don't think that'd be a..."

"Sure would, Ma'am. Thanks!" The agreement is from the skinnier of the two, with a sly grin on his lips. He reminds me of a big prankster. I instantly warm to him.

"Please call me Annabelle," I answer, standing back to let them in. There's a moment of fear as I hear my father's voice in my ear about trusting the wrong men and bringing disgrace on the family. I shake off those memories. I'm a grown woman now. It's time I start living my life and leaving the past behind me.

"Holy shit, it smells good in here!" The blond one says; and I was right, I really like him. The darker one cuffs him over the head.

"Show some respect to Sabre's woman!"

I stop, and despite the tingle of excitement the man's words bring, I need to set them straight.

"I'm not Sabre's girlfriend, we just met today. I was stranded. He was just being nice. I'm lucky he runs a garage."

"Sabre doesn't run a garage." I hear from behind as I go to the fridge to get them some drinks.

"I'm afraid all I have is water or soda? Well, I did make some peach tea this morning?"

"You make your own tea?" This time from the darker one.

"Well, yeah."

"Tea is good!" They both say it in unison.

I'm not sure what to make of the looks on their faces. I go ahead and fill two glasses with my tea and some ice from the dispenser. By the time I get it done they're sitting at the bar, so I slide the drinks over to them.

"Okay, I've got to know names here, I feel silly calling you the blond and dark one," I tell them to break the ice because the silence makes me feel a little awkward. To busy myself, I go back to putting dessert together. I'm making a chocolate lasagna and it has to freeze for an hour, so I might as well do that while the guys are cooling down.

"We've been called worse, but I'm Keys and this ugly fuc...guy is Shaft," he says already finishing his tea. He looks so forlorn at his empty glass that I get the pitcher from the fridge and bring it over to fill both of their glasses back up.

"Would you guys like to stay for supper?" I ask before I can second guess myself. I'm alone so often, and though I probably should be wary of having strangers in my house, something about these guys make me feel safe. It was the same feeling I got around Sabre, only with Sabre, it was more intense.

"Sure, let me just shoot a text to our road boss, we were supposed...speak of the devil," he adds as his phone starts ringing.

"Yo. *(Pause)* No, we're finished. Sabre's woman just invited us to eat with her. C'mon man, it'd be rude to say no. Besides, she makes her own tea and shit, you should taste it."

Again my face warms at being called Sabre's woman. Why does he keep saying that? Why do I like it so much?

"Hey, Peaches? Torch and Beast want to come over and eat too, is it cool?"

I blink. *Torch and Beast?* Still, he asked, and it'd be rude to say no. I was always taught to never be rude. Then again, I was always taught to never have strange men in my home, either, and now I will have four.

"They're all part of the club, Sabre would be cool with it," Shaft says and I don't know why that makes me feel better, but it does. "Sure, but I'm afraid it's just meatloaf and mashed potatoes, some corn, and I am going to make a...."

"They'll be here in ten," he cuts me off.

I decide to just go with it. After all, Sabre would approve. *Maybe I'm coming down with the flu?* I shrug it off and ask the question that's been on my mind since they introduced themselves.

"Now, I have to know, how did you get these names? Sabre? Keys? Shaft?"

The men look at each other for a minute and shrug. Shaft is

the first one to speak up. "Well, Sabre got his because he's freaky with knives. Like, I think he could kill a fly by throwing a knife from 100 feet away. Though some of the men say it's because he's like a sabre tooth tiger, once he bites into something, he really latches on. He doesn't let go until the problem is gone or solved, whichever."

I listen to him talk and put my dessert together without really paying attention. My mind pictures Sabre holding a knife and caressing the blade while he's talking to me, and my breath lodges in my throat. I try to concentrate on the dessert, but I'm still thinking over what Shaft said about Sabre. I can't help but be intrigued—even if I shouldn't be.

Brittany, my big tabby cat, picks that moment to come in. She sniffs around the feet of Keys and swishes her tail at him. When he doesn't take the hint, she grabs him with her claws, at the back of his leg. I've been on the receiving end of that little temper tantrum. It's never good, even if he is wearing jeans.

"Ow! Son of a bitch!" He growls looking down to where Brittany is meowing at him and waiting. I get the feeling he wants to kick her into next week. To his credit, he doesn't.

"That's Brittany. She doesn't like to be ignored. Sorry. If you pet her, she'll move on," I tell him, not bothering to admit that she'll just move on to Shaft. "Now, how did you get your name, Keys?" I ask and look up to see he's stroking Brittany behind the ear.

"There's not a car I can't hotwire and start. You named your cat Brittany?"

I begin to answer him and then stop, "Why would you need to hotwire a car?"

"Why wouldn't I?" He asks in return and looks so thoroughly confused, I let it go. "So then, how did you get the name Shaft? Was it because of mechanical work? Or did you really get into that TV show or movie?" The silence stretches for so long that once I put the top layer of cream topping on the dessert and move it to the freezer, I have to look at them. "Well?" I prompt.

Shaft looks like he almost blushes but says nothing and neither does Keys. I close the freezer and go back to the bar. "C'mon, tell me how you got your name?"

I was so intent on my guests that I failed to notice the door open. In walks two more men. I can only assume these are Torch and Beast. Holy hell. Where is this garage and how in the world did I miss it all this time? Do they not have one ugly man in the bunch? One man is big and brawny and has this shaggy beard. Normally, I'm not a beard kind of girl; right now I so am. He has on this white t-shirt my girlfriends in college used to refer to as wife-beaters. I always thought they were ugly; but somehow, he makes it look like the best thing a man could wear. He's covered in ink everywhere. I'm just assuming this is Beast because well, the name fits. The other guy is muscled for sure, but he's leaner and more...pretty. Still, he's sexy, there's no doubt about that. His hair is kind of long and falls over to one side, and it makes a woman want to run her fingers through it. I bet he got his name because women all over carry a torch for him.

"Peaches, this is Beast and Torch," Keys says, pointing to each one to confirm their identity and yeah, I was right. I smile at them and then decide, as big as they look, I better make more food. I pull out the dough I had rising earlier and start shaping rolls.

"Hello," I answer, feeling slightly intimidated with all four of them staring at me.

"What are we talking about?" Torch asks and before I can answer, Shaft does.

"Peaches wanted to know how I got my name."

"Oh, that's easy," Torch says.

"It is?" I ask before placing another roll in the pan. I go to preheat the oven and come back to my dough. I'm ignoring looking at the men because honestly, I'm feeling out of my element here. I wish Sabre were here and that's a strange thought to have.

"Yeah, Shaft here doesn't care where he puts his cock. Beast once told him he'd put his shaft in a black snake's mouth if someone would hold it open. The name just stuck," Torch speaks up. I stop to think about what he said. My parents would be scandalized. I throw my head back in laughter. It feels strange...but, it feels good, too. I think I like being around Sabre's men.

5

SABRE

MINE. THAT'S A FOUR LETTER WORD YOU BETTER LEARN
REALLY QUICK. BECAUSE I PROMISE YOU, I WILL FUCK YOU
UP IF YOU TOUCH MY PROPERTY.

Before I even get to the front of the door, I hear the laughter and that just fucking pisses me off. I'm going to fucking beat down these motherfuckers. I sent two men to fix a damn vehicle, not move in on my property. Annie is my property. I don't give a fuck if I haven't said more than a handful of words to her. I want her, I saw her, and she's mine. I don't have to be fucking logical; I've never been before. I wrench open the door and stand there watching these sons of bitches hovering over my woman, and I swear, steam is coming out of the top of my head.

Annie is standing behind the bar in her kitchen and Torch, Beast, Shaft, and Keys are all sitting on the side closest to me in the large living area. They're eating dinner like it's an everyday occurrence and laughing. Fuck, even Beast is laughing, and I haven't seen that out of him in years. Annie is putting a glass in front of Keys and I watch as he grabs her hand, brings it to his lips and kisses it.

"Marry me, Annie! Marry me and make me the happiest man on the face of the Earth," he says in some fake ass voice. Instantly everyone is laughing, including Annie. *Her eyes sparkle.* I can see them from here, they fucking glimmer like stars, and she's laughing for some other motherfucker that is *not* me. That is *not* happening. In fact, this entire fucking scene is not happening. No way. *No-motherfucking-way.*

"What the actual fuck?"

Everyone stops laughing, instantly, and they should because I'm going to fucking kill some pretty-boy bikers, and I'm starting with that son of a bitch, Keys.

"Sabre! I didn't know you were going to come by. Did you bring the bill? Because your men here didn't, and I wanted to make sure..."

"We're not his men, love," Torch speaks up, and I instantly add him next on the list for calling Annie that dopey-ass nickname.

"You're not? But I just assumed you all worked at the garage."

"Garage?" Beast asks, his gruff voice echoing in the air.

I pinch my nose from the tension I can feel behind my eyes, take a deep breath, and then look back up.

"What are you motherfucker's doing in my woman's house?" The room goes silent, except for Annie's startled gasp. The men look at Annie and back at me.

"Peaches here made us dinner. Good thing you claimed her because if you hadn't, I was going to," Torch says taking a bite of food and watching me very closely. Motherfucker knows he's walking on thin ice.

"You would have had to get in line. I was just about to claim Peaches here myself," Beast says, and I look at him like he's lost his damn mind. Only trouble is, I can tell he's completely serious, and that's fucked up. My brother hasn't touched another woman since he lost his old lady, and that was almost two years ago.

"Wait, no one has claimed me. I don't think..."

"Hell, Sabre, is that true? Because if you haven't claimed her and she is open game, then I'm standing up right now saying that I'm staking her out, too," Torch says.

"Me too," Beast adds.

"Yeah, so am I," Shaft speaks up.

"Shut up prospect, this is none of your concern. Patched in members get dibs always motherfucker," Beast grumbles. Shaft gives him the one fingered salute but wisely doesn't argue further.

"She's mine. It's not even a question. The only question is what the fuck you yahoos are doing here?"

"Sabre..."

"Hush it, Annie. We'll discuss this after these idiots leave."

"Sabre, that's not being nice. I was feeding them dinner."

"Yeah, Sabre. Peaches is feeding us dinner."

"And that's another fucking thing. Why the hell are you assholes calling her Peaches?"

"We've decided that's her club name."

"The fuck you have," I growl, mad as hell. Even if I was going to call her that, it was mine to name her.

"You snooze you lose, brother," Torch says smoothly and that does it. *That pushes me over the edge.*

I walk to him and give him a punch in the gut. He sees it coming, so it's not like he's unprepared. In fact, he's expecting it because I don't even get to blink and he plants a fist into my jaw. I stagger backwards but manage to grab him by the shirt. I draw my fist back to mess up his pretty-boy smile when I'm blindsided by a broom. It slams me on the side of the face; the straw bristles poking into the skin. I step back to figure out what the fuck just happened, and that's when I see Annie holding the broom and those beautiful blue eyes pointing daggers at me.

"Stop hurting Torch! I won't stand for fighting in my house. Now, if you'd like to eat..."

Stop hurting Torch? She won't stand? The men are laughing in the background, but I don't take the time to give them the beat down they deserve. I grab the broom and throw the damn thing across the room. I hear it bang against something, but I don't turn around to see what. I grab Annie under her legs, throw her over my shoulder, and stomp in the direction of the hallway I saw when I came in.

"Stop it! What are you doing? Where are you going?"

"Bedroom. Where's your fucking bedroom, Annie?"

"What? You can't be serious. I demand you put me down right now! Sabre…"

She drones on, but I tune her out. I open the first door I come to and it's a bathroom. The second seems to be her bedroom. It's got dark brown walls and a dark purple cover on the bed, with lighter purple throw pillows. The curtains on the one large window are purple and the bed is a rich cherry color and huge. A fucking king-size, four-poster bed draped in silk and it all looks like it was made to fuck in. My Annie is full of surprises. Here I was expecting yellow daisies everywhere and a room so bright it would make my eyes hurt.

I stomp over to the bed and throw Annie down on it. She struggles to prop herself up on her elbows.

"I don't think…"

"Shut it, Annie, and roll over," I growl at her, taking my favorite knife out of the holster on my side.

Her eyes grow wide in fear and she rolls over. There are tears in her eyes, and I'm enough of a bastard that my cock gets even harder at the sight. She rolls over and that perfectly plump, round ass stares as me, and I want to jerk off right then and there. This isn't about me, though. Annie doesn't realize that she's mine. I'm about to give her lesson number one.

I place a knee on the bed and stretch out alongside her. I want her naked, but I'll do that tonight. For now, I just need one part of her naked. I move my hand along her thigh, smiling at how she jumps under my touch. I slowly move my hand up to capture her ass and massage one of the cheeks, loving the way the juicy flesh rolls in my hand.

"Sabre, don't hurt me…"

You can tell she's full of fear and her voice betrays her unshed tears and physical strain. That shouldn't turn me the fuck on, but it does. I reach and pull the clasp out of her hair and smile as the white gold falls over her back and onto the silky cover we're lying on. I pull her hair, not like I want to—not like I will. I apply just enough pressure so she can feel the sting and then I move it away from her ear.

"I'll never hurt you, Annie. In fact, if you ever feel like I am, all you have to say to get me to stop is ketchup."

"Ketchup?" She asks, her voice small.

"That's it, but you can only use that word if you think I'm actually going to hurt you. Using it any other time? That will cause problems. Do you understand, Annie?"

"Yes..." her voice squeaks out. It might be because my hand has moved under her pants now. She's so soft and warm, and I hate the panties she has on, even without looking at them.

"Now, what's your safe word?"

"Ketchup?" she asks, and I can't stop the grin that spreads on my face.

"That's it. Now, Annie, did you know that what you just did in front of my men was disrespectful?"

"What? How? You were hurting Torch, and I..."

I sigh heavily, sounding upset. In truth, I'm enjoying the hell out of this. Sweet Annie is going to be fun to teach.

I pull away from her. I take my forgotten knife and place it on her pants, using my hand to pull it away from her body and provide tension. Then I slide down the leg, easily separating the cloth.

"Ketchup!" Annie cries out and I sigh, this time I am annoyed. I ignore her and do the other sides of her pants the same way. "Ketchup!" She screams louder. I push the torn article down to her knees. She's wearing cotton briefs, plain white. If I were going to allow her to wear panties, this would be disappointing. I quickly cut into the side of them and roughly pull on them so they completely leave her body. Then, I throw them to the floor and admire what is mine. "Ketchup!" She screams again, and this time I decide I can't ignore her anymore.

"Annie, did you really think I was going to hurt you?" I ask her, my voice full of regret and disappointment.

"You destroyed my clothes!" She says and her voice is wobbly, but I also hear a thread of anger. Interesting.

"What did I tell you, Annie?"

"To say ketchup and you'd stop. But I did and you didn't, and I don't think…"

She's rambling and the further she goes, I don't hear fear in her at all. *At. All.* I hear anger and maybe a touch of excitement. So, I stop her tirade by sliding my hand against the opening of her pussy, not pushing my fingers in but applying pressure. She stops talking, and I think she stops breathing. Again, I'm smiling. *Son of a bitch.*

"Did the knife touch you, sweet Annie?"

"Knife?" She pants.

"Did it touch you?"

"N…n…n…no."

"Repeat after me, Annie. Sabre will…"

"Sabre will," she repeats.

"Not hurt me," I finish.

"Not hurt me."

I kiss her lower back in reward for being such a good girl. I then decide she needs a little more incentive and slide the tips of my fingers into her wet pussy. It takes all of my willpower to not slide into her further, to stretch her opening with my fingers and ready her for my cock. I don't. That's not in the plan right now

"Good girl. You're mine now, do you understand that, Annie?"

"I…we just met…"

I take my hand from her pussy and smack her ass hard. "You're mine now. Say it."

"Ow! Sabre!" I spank her again. When she doesn't answer again, I spank yet another time. And another. Another and finally another, her ass is red with my handprint. She's still not saying anything. More importantly, she has yet to say her safe word. She's also arcing her ass up to meet my hand, silently begging for more. I pet her beautiful, pink ass and wait. I need the words. It's silent for a few minutes, except for her ragged breath. I'm about to give up hope she will give me what I want. Then she speaks, "I'm yours."

6

ANNIE

I COULD BLAME IT ON CONFUSION. I'D BE LYING. WHATEVER
IS HAPPENING, I WANT. I DON'T KNOW WHAT WILL HAPPEN
NEXT, MAYBE THAT'S PART OF THE APPEAL.

"That's a good girl. I think you need a reward, sweet Annie," he purrs from behind me, his warm breath brushing my hair and teasing the skin exposed on my neck. Chills of excitement scatter down my spine. I'm having trouble catching my breath and have no idea what I'm doing. All I do know is that I'm excited. I want more. Maybe I've always had this inside of me and have just buried it, kept a tight leash on that side of me because of my parent's demands. Maybe I am just a whore, a scarlet woman as my dad calls them. It doesn't matter to me that I've only met Sabre. It doesn't bother me that we've barely spoken. I'd be a hypocrite to deny that my body likes what he's doing to me—that *I* like what he is doing. So when he whispers roll over to me in that dark voice, laced with filthy unspoken promises, I do it.

It's only then I remember he has cut away my underwear. I try to move my hands down to cover myself, but he grabs them. He takes a piece of my yoga pants that he cut off of me and wraps the soft cotton around my right wrist, then he positions it so I'm tied to the bedpost.

"What's your safe word, Annie?" He asks, his voice dark and foreboding.

"Uh...ketchup," I say turning my head to watch him tie my other arm to the opposite bedpost.

"Good girl, do you want to say your safe word, Annie?"

This should be the point where sanity comes back in. This should be the point where I scream the silly word ketchup at the top of my lungs—scream it so that they can hear me three states over. This is also where I should remember it's only been less than a few hours since I've known this guy. Where I should run these men out of my house, go to the local church and give my confession and beg forgiveness of my sins...What do I do? I give him the truth.

"Not even a little bit."

"Oh, that's my good girl, sweet Annie. I'm going to reward you for that. Do you want to be my good girl?"

"Yes..." I answer, squirming up to meet his hand that he's petting against the soft hair covering my female area.

"Hold still, sweetheart," he says, his lips gently kissing my neck and then further down, following an imaginary trail on my breast.

His teasing is almost too much, and my heart is hammering in my chest.

"Sabre please...touch me."

"Touch you where, Annie?"

"On...in my...you know where, Sabre."

"Tell me, I want to hear you say it," he growls against my skin right before he takes my nipple into his mouth. Even through my clothes it feels amazing. I want to demand he take my bra and shirt off so I can feel more. My hips thrust up and my body twists and turns to try to get close to him. I strain against the bindings on my wrists. He pulls away and shoves my shirt and bra over my breasts, exposing them to the cold air.

"Sabre!" I call out feeling as if I'm drowning in want...*in need*.

"Shh...you need to be quiet sweet, beautiful Annie. The boys are right outside and they can hear every sound you make."

I imagine that and my heart drums in my ears. I know it's all kinds of wrong, but thinking about the others listening excites me even more.

"Please, Sabre." I groan as he takes my breast into his mouth again. It feels amazing without my clothes in the way. His tongue darts over the nipple while he sucks hard and releases it with a pop.

"Tell me where you want me to touch you Annie, and I'll give you what you want, sweetheart."

He goes back to teasing my breast, torturing it with his tongue and capturing it between his teeth. I pull hard against my restraints wanting to grab his head or his hand, something to give me more. *I need more.* He bites down hard on my nipple and pulls, and I scream out before I can stop myself. "My cookie! Touch my cookie!"

I thought that would make him give me what I want. Instead, he stops everything and I growl out in frustration. I try to rip my hands free, but I can't. Then I feel the bed start shaking. I look down and Sabre has slid to the end of the bed and is looking at me, but he's also laughing. He's laughing loudly!

"Sabre?" I ask, slightly coming out of my sexual haze and starting to feel self-conscious. I don't know him. Not at all really. I let him tie me up! I let him touch me! There're strange men out in my living room! What in the world am I doing? What was I even thinking? "Ketchup!" I growl, pulling against the restraints. Sabre doesn't say anything in reply, I'm not even sure he heard me because he's laughing so hard. "I said ketchup!" I scream it out this time, there's no way he can't hear me.

"Shut it, Annie," he grumbles though there is still a smile on his face.

"Ketchup!" I scream louder, but that doesn't make him untie me. No, he does something I never realized men do, and something I never thought I would like. He spanks my lady parts...*hard*.

"I told you to only use that word if I was hurting you or you didn't like what I was doing to you. Did I hurt you?" he asks and his eyes are frozen on mine. I'm still stinging from his slap and my body remains half aroused, even if I'm not in the haze I was before.

"No..." I whisper truthfully, looking away from him and to the wall by the bed.

"Look at me, Annie. Did you like my mouth on you?"

"Yes..." I whisper, my attention captured by the dark look in his green eyes. They're glowing almost like jade glass. Beautiful is the word that pops into my mind, and they are.

"Then why did you use your safe word?"

"You were laughing at me..." I grumble, looking away again.

"Eyes on me, Annie. Eyes on me." I can't help but obey the command in his words. "I wasn't laughing at you, sweet Annie. I was laughing at what you called your pussy."

His frank words bring heat to my face and I look up at the ceiling.

"Annie," he growls.

"Yes?" I ask, still staring at the ceiling.

"Have you ever had a man inside that hot little body of yours?" he asks, and it should bother me, but it doesn't. It feels wicked talking with him about this, and it makes me feel alive. Maybe I'm being seduced by the devil.

"No..."

"So you're innocent? No man has ever fucked you? Has one ever made you come?"

"Sabre..." I shift on the bed, I'm not sure how words can excite me, but his manage to.

"Eyes, Annie."

"No..." I look at him and whisper my answer like it's a dirty secret. I'm scared it will turn him off to know that I have no idea what I'm doing here.

"Has a man ever had his mouth on you?"

"I...yeah. I've been kissed, but..."

"I don't mean your mouth, sweetheart."

I wait for him to explain, I have no idea what he wants from me.

"Fuck me, you are innocent. Do you want to know why I laughed so loud when you screamed out cookie?"

"I uh...I guess so...or not. I really, this isn't fun Sabre, I think maybe I should have thought this through more. I mean it's kind of insane. We don't know each other, we've barely spoken. I think I just got carried away because you're so good looking and things but well, I am not that kind of girl. I mean I guess you know that now of course, it's just..." I stop talking, rattling really, when he slaps me *there,* yet again.

"Now that I got your attention. I asked you a question. Answer it, Annie."

"I don't know. Why?" I ask and I sound petulant, like a child. I am pouting. I can't help it.

"Because, sweetheart, I've decided I'm going to be your own personal cookie monster."

I freeze, wondering if he means what I think he means. He looks so heart-stoppingly gorgeous taking me in with those beautiful eyes, his dirty-blond hair streaked naturally with lighter shades, his body so solid and defined, ink covering his arms and hands. Again, the word beautiful comes to mind. "My...what?" I ask, and that's when I lose it, completely. He gives me a half smile and it makes his eyes sparkle even more, and I think this is it. This. Is. It. It doesn't matter if I don't know him. It doesn't even matter if I just met him. I like him. I *want* him, and I don't want to pass this up. Sabre doesn't answer. Instead he pulls my legs apart, the whole time his eyes are on me. He uses his thumb to open me to him and

I heat up in embarrassment because no one has seen me like this before. Then he does something I may have read about in books, but I never expected to experience. He puts his face against my center and I feel his tongue slide through my slit and push against the delicate skin there and lick me like I was an ice cream. It's like nothing I've ever felt before, but something I definitely want to feel again. My eyes are drawn to his. My hands are tight against the restraints and I whisper the one word that I know deep inside he wants from me right now. I give it freely. *"Please."*

7

SABRE

I'VE SEEN SOME FUCKED-UP SHIT IN MY LIFE. IT'S SHAPED ME
AND MADE ME THE MAN I AM. I NEVER THOUGHT I'D EVER
SEE ANYTHING INNOCENT. I SURE AS HELL NEVER THOUGHT
I'D BE THE ONE TO TOUCH IT.

I hear her whisper please and that's all I need. I bite gently
along the inside of her thighs, teasing and licking. I tease
one of her breasts, rolling the nipple between my fingers
and tugging gently. Her pussy is beautiful. Fine blonde hair
covering it, delicate pale flesh, and the sweetest scent that calls to
me. It's like coming home.

I use my free hand to pull her tender little hood back, flatten
my tongue again and lick over her clit, taking a minute to suck it
into my mouth and then lashing it gently with my tongue before
letting it go. Her whimper of need above me tells me I'm on the
right track. I dart my tongue across her pussy, touching her everywhere, but never long and never with enough force to send her
over the edge. She's so responsive, I know instinctively this won't
take long. I like knowing she's that hot for me. I fucking love
knowing no other man has had this from her. She tastes of lazy
summer days, sweet, tart, and fresh. I slide my hand under her
leg, pulling her hard against my mouth. I zero in over her clit,
humming in approval as more sweet juice flows from her and I
drink it down. I break away briefly and my eyes find hers. Those

beautiful blue eyes are hazed with need and it's a look I want on her face all the time. I slip my fingers into my mouth while she's watching, making sure they are nice and wet and then push them inside her waiting pussy.

"Sabre!" She calls out loudly at my entry. I go back to teasing her clit with my tongue, smiling because I know those fuckers in the other room can hear her. I curl my fingers and start fucking her slowly with two of them, still using my tongue to worry the hard little nub that is jumping with the firm beating of her pulse. With my fingers leisurely sliding in and out, I make sure to put extra pressure on her clit with each inward thrust. I capture the nub between my teeth, pull, and then suck it hard, all while pushing my fingers as far as I can get them inside of her that she screams out the words that let me know she's a wildcat.

"Eat me! Oh god, don't stop, Sabre!"

In repayment for her plea, I stretch my fingers and arc them, while continuously licking her sweet pussy—from the point where my fingers disappear deep inside of her, to the top, and back again. I lap her up like a man dying of thirst, drinking in every ounce of sweetness she will give me. Her hips are thrusting high off the bed and she's grinding against my mouth. Her legs are wrapped around me, the heels of her feet pushing into my back. She's wild as hell with need. I can feel the nerves and muscles flutter beneath my tongue. I know she's close. I'm probably ten different kinds of fucked up and definitely a bastard, but I decide to do something I know will slow her down. I'm just not ready for this to end.

"Shhh... Annie, I need you to be quiet or my brothers outside will hear your sweet voice and know you're giving your pussy to me."

Her whole body tightens up, just as I knew it would.

"Sabre," she whispers frantically and I smile as I begin my onslaught again; finger fucking her, slow and steady in tandem with my tongue. I keep my line of vision on her, watch her head go back in pleasure and then slowly pull back up, watching me—watching everything I'm doing to her. I admire the fine mist of perspiration that covers her body, making her glow almost. My eyes move to her hands and I watch as she pulls on the bindings, trying to reach me even now, knowing it's impossible. She's completely at my mercy—completely owned by me. It's fucking beautiful, and my cock is throbbing to get inside of her. It's not going to happen. *Not yet.*

I push my thumb against her clit, hard, as I lick down the lips of her pussy and then bite. She growls and I grin, pulling on the skin I have trapped. I continue fucking her with my fingers, as my mouth moves to the tender area on the inside of her thigh. I feel the need to mark her. I'm not going to fuck her yet, but I need something to know my mark is on her. So I torment her all along her thigh, leaving love bites and bruises in my wake. With each one, I get rougher. Annie loves it. Her cries become louder and she's practically thrashing, demanding of her release. I look up at her beautiful face, and she bites into her lip and whimpers. I could do this all night, but those fuckers are out there, sitting around my woman's bar, eating my woman's food, and I want them gone. I sit up, her taste all over my face and lips. It's a flavor I could come to crave.

"You're so fucking gorgeous, Annie. Do you want to come, sweetheart? Do you want to fucking come all over my face?"

"Yes, oh god, please, Sabre."

"Then give me the words, Annie. Tell me to eat your pussy." I continue to finger fuck her slowly, needing her reply before I push her over the edge.

"Eat me please, Sabre. Don't stop," she moans and that's close, but not everything I'm searching for from her. I take my free hand and slap that pretty, swollen pussy hard as I thrust my fingers deep inside of her again. She cries out, and I repeat the action. I feel what that does to her in the way her muscles start clenching around my fingers and her sweet cream increases. I want to lick up every drop, but not until she gives me what I want.

"Say it, Annie. Give it to me and I'll make your sweet pussy come so hard you will feel it for hours," I promise, meaning every word.

She looks at the wall. She knows the men are just on the other side of it. She knows what I want, what I'm asking.

"Sabre, please..." she whispers.

"Give it to me, sweetheart," I urge.

"Eat my pussy," she says, and if she weren't already flushed from what we've been doing, I know she'd be blushing right now.

That's when I cave and give her what she needs. I slide down using my tongue and fingers to fuck her into complete submission. I stretch her slick cunt with my fingers and push my tongue inside. I eat her out with my face, using whatever I can to make her quake. Her pussy quivers and flutters against me, her muscles are constricting against my fingers so tight, I know she's close. I slide my thumb into her ass and push her over the edge. She comes hard, crying out so loud I know my brothers in the next room are hearing her. She shatters, calling out my name and cementing whatever this is. I've claimed her. I wasn't planning on keeping her. *Now, I am. Now, she's mine.*

I want to make her come again, but I don't. This was just to give her a taste. Let her know that I will rule her body—let my brothers know. I slowly take my fingers from her, placing a small kiss against the opening and allowing my tongue to drag in one last taste of her nectar.

I slide to the floor and get up regretfully. I walk around to the side of the bed, adjusting my cock, which is pushing against my jeans; my balls literally hurt with the need to come. Annie watches me, her eyes still drugged from her release. I bend down and kiss her, wondering how she will react to her taste on me.

Her kiss is hesitant at first, and then she groans as our tongues begin dancing with each other.

"Do you like the taste of your pussy, Annie?"

"Sabre..."

"Answer me, do you like the taste? Does it make you feel like a naughty, wicked, little girl knowing I tongue fucked you while four men were outside listening? Do you want me to fuck you again?"

She looks down at my chest and again bites into that plush lip of hers before answering.

"Yes. I liked it. I want it again. Are you going to give it to me?" She asks.

"Eventually, sweetheart. Not right now. Right now, I'm hungry and I want rid of those assholes in the other room," I tell her, giving her one last kiss.

I untie her wrist, kissing it gently, then do the same with the other one. She grabs the edge of the comforter she's been lying on to try and cover her body. I don't let her.

"Never try to hide your body from me, Annie. You gave it to me in here today. I'll take care of it. It's *mine*—you are mine now."

"Sabre, what just happened in here..."

"Sealed your fate," I tell her, stopping whatever she was about to say. I bend down and kiss her hard, my tongue owning her mouth. When she starts to pull me closer to her, her nails biting into my back, I pull away.

"Oh, it also did one other thing," I tell her, opening the door to her bedroom.

"What's that?" She asks me, and I notice she has covered up again. I figure I might as well teach her a lesson now. I leave the door open and walk back to her. I flip her over on the bed quickly, making sure not to hurt her. The open palm of my hand connects with her ass three times, in quick succession. She squeals, but by the third time, her ass is pushing up—needing more. I reach under her to hold her warm, wet pussy against my hand.

"I said, not to cover yourself up. Didn't you hear me, Peaches?"

"I...I thought you were leaving," she gasps. I lift her ass using the hold I have on her pussy and bend down so I can bite her ass and suck on the skin. I want my mark on it. Hell, I'm going to tattoo my name all over her body.

"I hadn't left yet. For your punishment, do not wear panties when you come back to the kitchen."

"What? But, Sabre!"

I still have one hand wrapped around her pussy and feel the liquid heat there. I use my other one to push my thumb against the small rosette of her ass. She gasps and tightens up. I'm pretty sure she's a virgin, she's too damn tight and closed up to be anything else, but she doesn't tell me to stop. *Mine.*

"Do you want me to make you come again, later?" I wait for her answer, continuing to play with her ass. When she nods her head yes, I let her pussy go slowly, dragging one finger in the cleft between the lips and lowering her back on the bed.

"Then don't wear your panties," I order getting ready to leave again. I decide not to wash up. Let the bastards smell her on me. I like that thought. I'm almost out the door when her voice stops me.

"What was the other thing you were going to tell me?" She asks.

I look around and she's not hiding. She's still lying on her stomach, and not making an effort to cover up. I take it as a small victory.

"I've decided to let the nickname of Peaches stand," I tell her with a grin.

"Peaches? You didn't like them calling me that?"

"No, I didn't like them naming my woman, but I've decided to let it stand."

"Why?"

"Because I'm the only one who knows that you really are juicy and taste like peaches. Those other dumb fucks are just talking out of their ass."

She inhales at my answer, her eyes round.

"Remember, Peaches, no panties," I order, and then close the door with a smile.

8

ANNIE

WHAT DID I JUST DO? WHEN CAN I DO IT AGAIN?

He closes the door and I bury my head into the mattress. I can't believe I just did that and with a man I don't even know! Except it doesn't feel like we're strangers. I roll over on my back, dragging the comforter over me and stare up at the ceiling. What am I doing here?

My father is an evangelical preacher. An extremely devout one. He used to beat me until I couldn't sit down or lie on my back from the punishment I received. There are thin spiderweb-like scars on my lower back and side from the belt he used. Sabre either didn't take time to notice them, or he didn't really care about them. I'm hoping it's the latter. Having Sabre and the men here would send my father into a rage. If he knew what I did with Sabre, he would kill us both. In my father's eyes, what Sabre and I did would be sinning and reveling in our fall from grace. It would be in direct violation of God's commandments.

My stomach lurches at the reminder of my father. He is in Illinois, and his teachings have never been my beliefs. What kind of God would find it okay for a father to use a belt on his eight-year-old daughter because the boy next door held her hand on the way home from school? What kind of God would condone a man who cut all his daughter's hair off because he thought she was using it to lure boys into her bed?

I tap down those memories. *I got away.* I moved to Kentucky. I no longer have to live in fear. Admittedly, it only happened because I got a job offer here and my father's brother lives in the same town so he can report back to my father. Carl can never know about Sabre. *Ever.*

I hear laughing from the other room and sigh. I need to get up and go out there before Sabre comes and finds me. Maybe it's because I'm just now getting my first taste of freedom as a woman, I just don't know, but I know I want more time with Sabre. I like him, or rather I like what I know of him, and the rest of the men seem nice, too. So I'm going to throw caution to the wind and enjoy this for however long it lasts.

With my mind made up, I go into the adjoining bathroom, clean up, search out some comfortable clothes, and return to the kitchen. My face flames with embarrassment as everyone stops talking when I enter the room. I'm having trouble looking any of them in the eye.

"Over here, Peaches."

Sabre is standing in the kitchen on the opposite side of the others and he looks very pleased with himself. It annoys me, but I had a lot to do with putting that look on his face. I walk to him and when I get there, he takes me in his arms. I return his hug and then let him curl me into his side. I like it. I like how it feels to be with him.

"Hey, Peaches. We were starting to think you weren't going to join us," Keys speaks up and I give him a small smile without looking him directly in the eye.

"Have you eaten?" I ask Sabre.

"Nah, sweetheart. I'll get something in a bit," he answers, and I grasp at it. I need something to keep busy.

"I'll get it. Just pull up that seat over there. We all should have eaten at the table. There's more room there. I never use the darn thing personally, so it didn't occur to me. Next time, well if there is one, I will set it up..."

"Peaches?" Sabre interrupts my sad rambling and I'm glad. I look up at him in mid-sentence.

"Stop being nervous."

I huff in response, "Sabre, you can't just order someone to not be nervous."

"I just did," he says all cocky.

"Well okay, you can order someone to do it. That, however, doesn't mean they will do it."

"Did you do as I ordered in the bedroom?" He asks as if he's talking about the weather. It doesn't escape my notice that everyone has gone quiet again.

"Sabre!"

"Answer me."

"That isn't something you just talk about in mixed company," I chastise getting a plate down and filling it up with what is left of the meatloaf and side items.

"What's she calling us? Does she not like other races?" Shaft asks, and he is clearly Latino.

"No dumbass, she's just saying she doesn't want to talk about how her and Sabre had sex in front of a bunch of men," Beast growls and I probably glows in the dark. I put the plate down without looking at any of them and go back to the fridge to get Sabre something to drink. I think at this point, I'd rather pour it on him.

"We weren't in front of a bunch of men," I grumble, but I don't think they are listening to me.

"For god's sake, why? We all sat here and listened to her scream like a banshee as he laid the pipe to her," Shaft asks and my head jerks up with an unspoken *oh* on my lips. I can't believe he said that. I'm rewarded when Torch slaps him on the back of the head.

"Ow! What the fuck is that for?"

"You're embarrassing, Peaches," he says looking up at me with a wink and licking some of the chocolate off his spoon.

I guess the boys found the chocolate lasagna. I can't help but watch the way Torch works his tongue around the spoon and sucks it into his mouth. He's a really good looking man and, apparently, I've just recently found my hormones.

"Peaches!" Sabre snarls and stops my crazy thoughts. I go to him immediately and he pulls me back against his body. "You'll pay for that later, sweetheart," he whispers into my ear.

I don't have to ask what he means—I know. It's not like I would trade him for Torch, anyway. *I was just looking.* I reach up and kiss him on the side of his jaw. His five o'clock shadow prickles against my lips. It's a good feeling. I start to pull away but he keeps me close, anchoring me against him.

"Why does she care if we talk about her having sex? I mean why else would she be screaming ketchup at the top of her lungs? By the way, brother, you really need better safe words. That one is kind of freaky. That's worse than the time you guys had that redhead screaming cheeseburger and Skull thought..."

This time Sabre slaps Shaft up the side of the head. I don't mind. I kind of want to join in. His words leave me feeling *dirty*, wrong even.

"Okay, it's time for everyone to get out," Sabre yells and he's mad; he won't let go of me. Maybe he can tell that if he let me go, there is a very big possibility that I would go get in my car and drive back to Illinois. Okay, maybe not that drastic but away just the same.

"C'mon Sabre, we haven't even had any cookies yet," Keys joins in and they all look at me, and if you could spontaneously combust, well, I'd be doing it right now.

"Get out you fucking assholes. Beast? Have these prospects cleaning out the bathrooms at The Rock."

"With pleasure. Great food, Peaches. Look forward to seeing you around," Beast grumbles. I don't think he can talk any other way. He grabs Shaft and Keys by their collars at the back of their neck and pretty much pulls them out of the room. They're too busy whining over having to clean bathrooms to do much else. Beast is so big that he handles the large men rather easily.

Torch comes over and picks up my hand and kisses the back of it, despite Sabre pushing him away. "Until next time, love," he says with another wink.

"Keep your motherfucking hands away from her," Sabre warns him, but it doesn't seem to bother Torch at all.

And just like that—we're alone.

"Sabre, I think maybe you should go, too."

"Did you mind me?" he asks and I blanch at the words. Does he think I'm a mindless child who will do everything he commands?

"I have no idea what you..."

"Are you wearing panties, Peaches?"

"I...uh...well, no."

"Good girl. Now let's finish eating, I'm starved."

"It's kind of cold now," I answer him, wondering exactly what twilight zone I've slipped into.

"So we'll zap it in the microwave. C'mon Peaches, feed your man," he says walking into the kitchen.

My man? Maybe I have fallen off the deep end. I follow him into the kitchen and help nuke his food. I get a little bit for myself and sit beside him. We don't really talk, but it doesn't feel awkward. Something is bothering me, though, so instead of pushing my mashed potatoes around in the plate, I decide to ask him.

"Shaft made it sound, like well..."

"Spit it out, Peaches."

"He made it sound like you guys, shared...like well...he mentioned a red-head and it sounded like...well..."

"We share women from time to time."

"Share? Like once you date one, sometimes they go out with

Torch, too?"

"You need to get that motherfucker, Torch, out of your head right now," he growls and his voice is full of anger.

"I wasn't, I mean I wasn't thinking that I would, you know…"

"Damn, Peaches, can you say any actual words?"

"I think you should go now. I can say *those* words," I retort carrying our plates into the kitchen. Sabre gives a loud sigh in the background.

"The brothers and I don't date, Peaches. He's talking about a club girl. They hang around the club, live the life. They help us release steam, take care of our needs, and we do the same for them."

"I thought you ran a garage…"

"You thought wrong," he says mysteriously.

"What is it you do?" I ask, clenching my hands into a fist.

"I'm a member of the Devil's Blaze Motorcycle Club."

"But what do you do?" I ask, looking at him in shock. I'm such a fool. I let this man touch me and I know nothing about him. Maybe my parents are right, I'm not ready for the real world.

"That is what I do," he answers and I don't question him further. Something in his stance tells me that asking would only annoy him.

"I'm not the kind of girl who dates bikers," I say before I can stop the words.

"The way I look at it Peaches, you don't know what kind of girl you are yet. I'm going to help you figure that out."

Maybe he does have me pegged.

"I don't want to be shared with other men, Sabre. If that's what you want, then you should leave."

"We'll never do anything you don't want to do, Peaches."

I'm pretty sure Sabre is the king of cryptic answers.

"You're not staying the night. We need to slow this down."

"We'll see," he says taking a bite of his food.

Crap.

9

SABRE

A MAN CAN ONLY TAKE SO MUCH. SHE WANTED TO GO
SLOW. I GAVE HER A WEEK, BUT A SAINT COULDN'T TAKE
THIS SHIT.

nnie asked me to slow things down. She had a look of panic in her eyes, so I backed off. Well, I haven't fucked her yet. That's as much backing as I'm capable of doing. She's still in my arms every night, and I'm still at her house having dinner and spending time with her. It's almost like a white picket fence type of life, except I'm not fucking cut out for that. I'm living a fucking lie with her and that's burning a hole in my craw. I'm going to have to bring her into my world, there's no other way about it because I'm sure as hell not letting her go.

"Hey, Peaches," I say, walking up behind her and wrapping my arms around her and my mouth whispering against her neck. We're standing outside of the library. She just got off work and she's wearing this pale pink skirt with a matching silk blouse under a pink sweater and some more fuck-me heels. Yeah, I'm going to make her leave those shoes on tonight. It's time to dirty up my girl even more.

"Sabre," she whispers back and I might not be able to see it, but I hear the joy in her voice and feel the way her body instantly relaxes back into me. Her plush ass rubs against my groin and my cock protests. Poor guy is going to be permanently blue if he doesn't get relief soon. That's another reason I'm done with waiting. I'm dying to be inside her. Fucking hell, I've jacked off so many times this week my hands are getting calluses.

"I've missed you today, my sweet Annie."

"I missed you, too," she exhales because my hand reaches between us and kneads that gorgeous ass of hers.

"You ready to go?" I ask her, anxious to get home. It's Friday and I plan on fucking her all weekend long.

She nods her head yes, and we walk towards my old beat up Ford.

"Where's your bike?" she asks, and I like the disappointment in her voice. Peaches doesn't know it just yet, but she has all the makings of being a fucking fantastic ole' lady, I just have to help her tap into it.

"Weatherman said it was going to rain," I lie, opening the door for her and groaning when the tight material of her skirt stretches over that fuckable ass. She looks up at the sunny-not-a-cloud-in-sight sky but doesn't say anything. Then she hops inside the truck. I get behind the wheel and wait until I have us out on the main road before I put my plan into action.

"Come sit beside me Peaches, I've missed you."

"You just saw me over breakfast this morning," she argues but slides over just the same. Her skirt rises up on her thigh, exposing more delicious skin and my dick is practically vibrating. If he doesn't get in her pussy tonight, he'll probably shrivel up and die from starvation.

"I had you for breakfast this morning," I rumble. Just because my dick isn't getting action, doesn't mean I can't keep warming her up. The way I figure it, the more her body craves release only I can give her, the fucking better. I glance over at her to see her blush. She's special. Her innocence calls to the hardened man inside of me.

"I remember, Sabre," she says, lying her head on my shoulder.

"Did you remember the rule?"

"You really are insane you know. I'm in a library all day. Do you know how many people come in and out of there all day?"

"So you ignored what I asked?"

"I didn't wear underwear, okay? And it was extremely uncomfortable. I'm trying to figure out why I even like the things you have me do."

"But you do. Admit it, Peaches."

She's silent, and I figure she's going to back down and then she surprises me, "I do."

I slide my hand up her leg and under her skirt; warm, wet heat greets my fingers.

"Sabre!"

I ignore her and move so my fingers slide between the lips of her pussy. Her muscles tighten under my hand, but she spreads her legs slightly to signal she wants more.

"I've missed this warm little pussy today. Did you get the video I sent you on your phone?"

"Yes..."

"Did you watch it?"

"Yes, I watched it."

"Did it make you horny, Annie? Did you get all excited and wet watching that chick sucking cock while her man fucked her from behind?"

"I shouldn't be watching things like that. My parents would exorcise demons out of me if they knew I watched that."

I grin, I can't help it. She's told me a little about her fucked up parents. It's sadistic, but it makes it more enjoyable. I ever meet that fucker of a father, I might just kill him. When I questioned her about the scars on her back and she admitted her dad beat her, I wanted to go to Illinois right then.

"Did you get wet, sweet Annie? Did you need to be fucked? Did you want to come?"

"I, uh...yes."

Something in her voice alerts me. Oh, my little Annie has

been a bad, bad girl.

"Did you make yourself come?"

"Sabre!" She protests, but she doesn't answer me. My hand bites into her tender flesh on her thigh, and I ask again.

"Did you make yourself come, Annie? Answer me."

"I..."

"Annie, do not lie to me."

"I...yes. I did. It was...I mean, I read and things, but I never read a book where there were three people involved, and I never thought it'd be so...."

"Hot?"

"They both wanted her. They needed her, it was kind of like she had power over them, even when they were rough and..."

"Fucking her so hard she screamed?"

"I...yes..."

"Tell me what your favorite part was. Be honest."

The truck is quiet except for the sound of the engine and the wheels rolling along the highway, but even over that I can hear Annie's breathing. She's just a step away from coming and I've barely done more than pet her sweet little snatch.

"When he bent her over her desk and made love to her while his buddy watched."

"Oh, Annie, that wasn't making love, that was fucking. He fucked her. Say it."

"He fucked her..."

"We have a problem though, sweet Annie."

"Why am I Peaches sometimes and Annie others?" She asks out of the blue, and I think to dodge what she knows is coming next. *She's cute.*

"Because you've been named Peaches by the club, but you're my Annie. That's why when I'm eating you out I only use Annie. When I'm not fucking you or eating you? You can be both to me. But no other motherfucker better say your name from here out. It's mine."

She remains silent, shifting in the seat. It doesn't escape my attention how she bucks against my hand, wanting more.

"Sabre, I need..."

"Sorry, baby. That can't happen, you were a bad girl."

"But...you told me to watch it. I never would have..."

"I don't mean that Annie. I mean you didn't have permission to make yourself come. Your pussy belongs to me now. No one makes that pussy come but me or unless they have permission from me."

"Explain again why I like the things you do to me?"

"Because there's a wild woman inside of you, sweet Annie, and you like her. Now, I'm afraid you're going to have to be punished."

"Punished?" she questions, and I can hear the fear in her voice and really wish her fucking father was closer. I pull off to the side of the road then put my hand under her chin and pull her closer. I make sure our eyes connect; I need her to understand this.

"I would never hurt you, Annie. You're important to me. The more time I spend with you, the more I want. You get that, right?"

"Yes, I feel the same, Sabre..."

"Ultimately, when I punish you, it will be to teach you what pleases me, but it will also be about teaching you what brings you pleasure. You understand?"

"Not completely, but I think I get the gist."

I kiss her forehead. "Trust me, Annie. Eventually, you might just seek out punishment from me."

"What is my punishment now?"

"The video I sent you? Did you watch as she sucked on that man's cock?"

"Yeah..."

"You're going to suck me off just like that, and if you're a good girl, I'll come in your mouth and not all over your face like I want to."

"I...I've never done that. What if I disappoint you?"

"Sweetheart, nothing you could possibly do will disappoint me. Take your time, experiment, learn what I like. You will figure it out."

She looks at me and nods with a slight smile. Innocent, pure, eager to please, and fucking hot as hell—that's my Annie.

"I'll do it as soon as we get home."

"That's not going to work for me, sweetheart. You're going to suck me right now," I tell her, unbuckling my jeans and releasing the button and zipper. My aching, hard cock springs out; the head already moist and ready for action. "Now angle yourself so the steering wheel isn't in the way and show me what you learned from the video," I instruct her. She looks out the windows and back at me.

"Sabre, anyone can see us..."

"I guess you better use that sweet mouth to keep my cock all covered then. Now do it."

She slides her glasses off and puts them in her purse. She takes off the pink sweater she has over the tight little camisole and puts that to the side. Annie has no fucking idea right now how sexy she is, but damn, I can already feel my balls tighten. She slides down the seat so she can reach my dick easily, and I stop her right before her lips reach my cock. I hear her huff of frustration and I'm right there with her, but there's one more thing I need.

"Take your hair down, Annie."

She doesn't even question me and I want to growl in victory. She reaches up and undoes the complicated knot and silky strands of blonde fall down over her shoulders. *Hot as fuck, and all mine.* She bends her head down and I wrap my hand in that thick, beautiful hair. Her hand grips my cock gently, and I smile. Eventually, I'll teach her that she won't hurt me, but we don't have the time or the room right now. I pull out on the road and she hesitates. I think she must see the need in my eyes though because the next thing I feel is her sweet, little tongue sliding along my cock. I groan in response. Her tongue slides down my shaft and teases my balls.

"Fuck, yeah baby, suck it in your mouth..." I groan, keeping my eyes on the road but wishing I could watch her. Shit, I may have to pull over and finish this. She trails her tongue back up my cock and then it darts along the head, picking up the pre-cum that has leaked out. The next thing I know, she swallows my cock down. My hand tightens in her hair harder in reflex. Had we been together longer, if she knew more, I'd fuck her mouth hard and take what I want. We'll get there slowly because I'm not letting her go. *Ever.* I pull up to a traffic light and say a small thanks that it is red so I can watch her.

She is sliding those sweet lips up and down on my cock, her hand is wrapped tight around the base and her tongue is teasing me and I know I'm going to blow soon. Annie must notice that we've stopped moving because she releases my cock with a soft popping noise and looks up at me. Her lips are swollen and wet, her eyes are smoky like they always get when she needs to come, and what hair is not in my grasp is in disarray around her face. She looks out my window and there's a man sitting beside us, looking in my window.

"Sabre," she whispers like it's a dirty secret. "There's a man in the passenger side of that car watching us."

I roll my window down and smile at her. "Then I guess you better give him a good show so he goes home and works his woman over real good."

I'm not sure what I had expected. It was a test and sweet Annie, she passed with flying colors because she groans and takes my entire cock in her mouth while massaging my balls.

"That's it baby suck that cock. Suck it good and when we get home, I'll fuck you until you can't move," I growl.

She proceeds to do just that. *Sweet Annie.* I was right. She's got everything to make the perfect ole' lady. *My ole' lady.*

10

ANNIE

I WANT TO SCREAM. I REALLY WANT TO SCREAM.

I'm sitting up, trying to fix my hair, but it's useless. I don't even care, really. I'm so turned on at this point, I'm about to scream. I need Sabre. He's like a drug I'm definitely addicted to and my entire system is craving more. I still have the taste of him in my mouth. I've heard women don't like it. The taste is too acidic or bitter, but I love Sabre's taste. I love knowing I brought him to that point all on my own, and I want more. He promised he was going to make love to me until I couldn't move, and I want him to make good on that promise. Well, he said fucking. I suppose that's what it is, but for me...it's making love. I know I've only known him a week. I let him claim me after one day, and I have zero experience with men to know how Sabre really feels about me. None of that matters. I know in my heart that Sabre is what I need in my life. He makes me happy, that's true, but the real truth is that with him, I feel like I am finally alive for the first time in my life. He makes me feel real, instead of just a shadow. I've been nothing but a shadow my whole life.

He pulls into my driveway and my heart is beating out of my chest. He's out and pulling me through the door before I can even blink. Picking me up in his strong arms, I squeal with a laugh, wrapping my arms around his neck. Our lips bump together clumsily, teeth clashing for a minute before he hits that spot where we get in sync and then our tongues are at war with each other. I slip one hand under his t-shirt, caressing the warm, soft skin. I let my nails graze him, applying slight pressure so he can feel me there; know that I need him. I push his shirt up and turn in his arms enough to get my head angled so I can lick his nipple in my mouth. I bite down on the little nub, capture it between my teeth while using my tongue to play with it.

Sabre groans, I feel his leg thrust up against my ass to brace me and I'm pushed against the wall of the outside of my house. Sabre's rummaging around for keys in his pocket, I think. I can't really tell unless I stop what I'm doing, and I don't want to. This past week with Sabre has been amazing, but I need and want more. *I'm ready.*

"Goddamn it, I am too! I just can't find the fucking key," Sabre groans as I suck harder on his nipple. I use my fingers to tease his other nipple, at the same time that I'm torturing the one in my mouth. I didn't even realize I had said the words out loud. "Annie, if you don't stop, I'm fucking you against the wall of the house."

"Yes, or fuck me from behind like in the film, Sabre. Bend me over the banister and make me yours," I urge him, my body on fire. I can't control my words, I don't try. I'm safe with Sabre and I'm not the preacher's daughter, afraid of her shadow. I'm a woman. I'm Sabre's woman.

I hear keys hit the porch. The sound of them falling makes me happy. Then Sabre has me standing, my legs unsteady, but I ignore them. I drop down to my knees, thankful I didn't button his pants back up and unzip him. We're out in the open and I should care, but I *love* it. The idea that any minute someone could see us excites me even more. I take his cock out and hold it in my hand. I look up at Sabre before I go further, wanting to see his eyes—to know I'm giving him what he wants. He's taken his leather cut off, the one that has his club's insignia on it and has it draped over the banister. I whimper as he takes my hair in his grasp and roughly pulls it to arch my head. Now it's him in control, and I love every minute of it. He removes my hand from his cock and guides it to my lips, slanting my head just the way he wants me. He's not gentle, and it's so hot. He was right I think, I am wild inside and need him to let that out of me. He moves his cock along my lips, painting them with his pre-cum. He pulls me up by my hair so I have to stretch from my knees. I brace myself on his hips as he leans down to meet me.

"You're going to suck my cock, Annie. Suck it like you are dying for it and show me just how bad you need to be fucked," he growls, and it is growling, in the truest sense of the word. It's also hot and just ramps up my excitement.

I don't see a problem with that. I am dying for it, if he'd just let me go, I'd show him....

"First, I want to taste myself on your lips," he says before giving me the hottest, wettest kiss he's ever given me. He devours my lips in his mouth, licking, sucking, and plundering them. When we break away, I gasp and then instantly turn my attention back to his cock.

I take him to the back of my throat and try to relax the muscles there, to take him further. I want all of him, but he seems wider, harder than he was in the car. I use my hand to roll his balls around, concentrating so much on what I'm doing that I don't hear the roar in the background. I should have, but I'm too far gone into the place that making love with Sabre always sends me. His hands tighten in my hair, the pressure and sting of his rough hold is delicious.

Finally, I get his whole cock in my mouth and I know it's not just my imagination; he is bigger. I'm too much of a novice to know if that's possible, but I know how he feels in my mouth and I almost can't fit him. I hum against his cock and I want to give him what he wants from me, but I can't. I don't get the chance because he takes over. He doesn't ask, he demands. He uses his hold on me to push me up and down on his cock. Why does that excite me even more? I do my best to give him what he wants but he stops and pulls me away.

"Sabre, please, I need it," I whine, sounding like a child being denied her favorite treat—because I am, damn it!

"Well, hello there querida, and here I was wondering why I caught my man with his pants down."

I look up to see a rough biker looking over the railing at us. He's got dark hair and darker eyes. He looks worn and sad, even if there is laughter in his eyes. He's not pretty or poster-sexy like Sabre, but he's dangerous and there's something about him just the same. I decide all that in a matter of seconds because I'm too busy wanting to die of shame.

Sabre releases my hair and I slide away from him. I look up at him almost afraid of what I'll see. He gives me a tight smile, tucking his cock back inside his pants even though it's really too big to fit comfortably. I have the strangest urge to kiss it against the now zipped jeans since I can see the outline perfectly. I ignore the voice of caution and do it. I mean they've already seen what was happening. My face may be beet red, but I'm going to ignore it. Sabre's hand comes down and pets the side of my head gently. It feels like a reward. Maybe that's why Brittany, my cat, always wants me to pet her. Because right there, even with other people around, I think I might be the happiest woman around.

Sabre helps me to my feet, pulls me close to him, and tucks my head under his chin. I bury my head in his chest and hug him tight.

"What the hell do you guys want?" He says and I bury my head more, partly from embarrassment—okay, mostly from that. Still, I like the feel of being surrounded by him, I like the smell of him, I like everything about being in his arms.

"Aw, hermano! Do you not wish to introduce me to your new plaything?" The other man asks, and I want to disappear. I even think my heart hurts. I don't want to be a plaything. I've been fooling myself, I guess. I thought I was more.

"She's not a toy, Pres. Annie here is my ole' lady."

Everyone around us goes quiet. I pull back to look into Sabre's eyes. I'm not sure what the distinction is, but it feels important. It feels momentous. I want to savor it. To soak it in. I can't, though, because it hits me that over the past week, Sabre has explained how important his club is to him. He's told me how they are his family. He just basically made us a couple, and soon, I'm going to jump and scream and dance like a little girl over that. I want to scream it from the roof, but what is making me want to completely die of mortification is that I just met his President while on my knees sucking my man's cock.

I wanted to be Sabre's wild Annie. I wasn't exactly going for slut Annie.

Crap.

11

SABRE

COCK-BLOCKED BY MY OWN FUCKING CLUB. HELL, WHEN
DID GETTING INSIDE A WOMAN'S PUSSY TAKE AN ACT OF
CONGRESS?

I doubt Annie realizes the importance of what I just did, but
the boys do. Now, if they'd just fucking leave. From the look
on Skull's face, that's going to happen. If a man could go
stark raving mad from lack of pussy and being teased to death, I
am there. I am so fucking there. With a sigh, I let go of Annie and
reach over and get my cut, putting it back on.

"What's up?"

"Donahue brothers," Skull answers wearing that and the
haunted look again. I have an instant gut check moment. There's
not a brother among us that doesn't grieve for the loss of Beth.
There's not a brother who doesn't know the effect it's had on our
president. Skull is a different man.

"Where we headed?" I ask, knowing now why all the brothers
showed up on their bikes.

"Paradise Ridge," Skull says and my lips firm up in disgust.
Paradise Ridge is a spot on the back of a mountain where
Tennessee and Georgia meet. It used to be a place where
teenagers would park and make out, gaining it the name Paradise
Ridge because many a cherry was popped there. The Donahue
brothers claimed it not long after they took over as head of the

Irish faction in Georgia, and it's since become a place where bodies are buried and disposed of. "Who called the meeting?" I ask, my mind already turning from Annie to the long ride ahead of us.

"Colin," Skull says and that one name from his lips contains so much hate that it chills the air around us.

"Right. I'm ready. Let me say goodbye to my woman and I'll get my bike out of the garage." I had moved my bike and other things to Annie's in the past week. She's never said a word in protest, and I've known from that first sweet taste of her that I wasn't going anywhere. She's the one. Now, if I could just finally claim her completely, I'd be a happy fucking man.

"It was nice meeting you, querida. I am sure we will be seeing you around the club soon. Si?" Skull says and gives her a smile. Hell, even his smile is still cold. I look to Annie to see how she reacts. Damn, she's beautiful. Her hair is all messed up, her lips swollen, her nipples are poking through that silky little top she has on, and her pale skin sparkles in the sun. I'm a lucky bastard. She's got her hands wrapped around herself in a defensive gesture, but all it really does is point out the fact that's she's horny. A beautiful thing to behold for sure, but as I look around and see that all the brothers are watching, especially that mother-fucker, Torch, I take the one step to her and block her with my body.

"You are looking fucking hot, Annie. But if your nipples get any harder, every man around here is going to fall on you. Maybe you should go inside."

She inhales and her cheeks blush even darker. She starts to pull away and I stop her. "I'll be gone for a couple days. I'm going to send one of my brother's out here to check in on you and make sure you're safe. Try not to get him twisted up in knots over you, yeah?"

"Sabre! I would never do that, I can't believe..."

I stop her tirade with a hot kiss, not giving her time to

respond, just devouring her and letting my tongue pillage every part of her mouth. I can still taste my flavor on her and my damn balls seem to pulse with the need to come. My lips break from her mouth and kiss up her cheekbone and down into the valley of her neck before finally ending at her ear.

"You don't have to do a goddamn thing sweetheart, just the look of you is enough to make a man come. I'm a lucky bastard, and I know it. I just want those other men to know you're mine, too. Got it?"

I pull back away and she gives me this sexy smile and even I can tell she's happy. Mission accomplished.

"Be safe, please?"

I nod, satisfied with her reaction. She could have asked a million questions, she could have demanded to know what was going on. Her not doing so is just another sign that she will fit into club life perfectly. I've made a great decision, which is good because I'm starting to really care about this woman. I've always known from my first look that no other woman would ever compare. Now, I'm starting to think it's even more.

"You got it, Peaches, and when I get back, you and I have some unfinished business."

"I'll be looking forward to it," she smiles and it's that smile I take with me as I get on my bike.

~

It's about two in the morning when we reach the Tennessee, Georgia border. The crew is dog tired and none of us are looking forward to the meeting with Colin tomorrow. Colin is a bastard, though a few steps above his uncle who used to be in charge. We have a bad history with the Donahue family and I wasn't expecting this meeting to be good. We're bedding down for the rest of the night at the Green Goose, an old outdated no-tell motel that looks like hell and smells stale and that's about the nicest thing I can say about it. The mattress lays like it's been stuffed with straw and the occasional rock. I'm bunking down for the night with Skull. He's in the opposite bed holding the locket in his hands that he always wears around his neck. It was Beth's locket. A present he gave her on their wedding day. He's never once taken it off since Beth's funeral.

"What are you thinking Pres?" I ask him, trying to drag him out of the thoughts in his own head.

"How old ghosts never stop haunting you, amigo. They never do."

"Beth wouldn't want you to live your life like this," I tell him, knowing it's true. Beth loved Skull, she'd want him to move on and be happy.

"Love is a funny thing. It starts with a touch and burrows down under the skin, infecting your blood and ultimately your heart. It never lets you go hermano, never. It can feed you and make you strong, nourish you and make you whole, or it can slowly destroy everything inside of you until the person you are withers and you are left but a shell. A sad, empty, old shell with nothing but memories of days you should have cherished more." Skull sets the locket down on the fake wood nightstand by the bed, lays down, and turns out his light. It jars me, I know today's meeting has destroyed him.

"Do you wish you hadn't met her?"

"At times, si. Then I remember."

"Remember?"

"That before Beth, I had no life anyway. Hold on to your woman, hermano. Hold on tight and enjoy while you can. El tiempo es corto."

Skull's mother was Spanish, not his dad. But, she raised him, he knows the language well. He sounds American as hell, but most of the time he slips into the other language. The club has become fluent, or at the very least has a grasp on what he is saying. *Time is short.* I lie in the dark and listen as, eventually, Skull's breathing evens out. I pull out my phone and text Annie.

Missing you tonight, sweetheart.

There's a brief lull. I figure she's already sound asleep. I'm just putting my phone down when a message comes through.

Miss you too, Sabre. Please be safe. Love you. Xoxo

Love. I don't know what that is really. I've never had it. Yet, I like the idea of Annie loving me. I like it a fuck of a lot.

Before I met Beth, I had no life anyway. I think on Skull's words. I think I'm starting to understand exactly what he means. I've never had someone to come home to before. Someone to worry about me and take care of me. Annie does all of that and more. I need to appreciate that, cherish it, and make sure it's safe. I sure as hell don't want to be grieving like Skull does. I grab my phone and text Latch, a patched in member of the club who doesn't go on runs and shit. He's got a little sister at home he takes care of; she's only sixteen and Latch is her only family. They lost their mother a year ago to breast cancer. Latch and I are tight. We have a connection the other brothers don't know about and would never understand.

Me: *You keeping an eye on my woman?*

My phone vibrates a few minutes later.

Latch: *Outside her house right now. Never fear.*

Me: *Everything cool?*

Latch: *She got a visit from an uncle, today. Carl something. It seemed to freak her out. I'm keeping a close eye.*

Me: *Do that. I'll check in tomorrow.*

Latch: *I'm on it. Later.*

I don't like the idea of Annie having problems with me so far away. If her uncle is anything like her father, I know why she is upset. I'll have to call her in the morning. I roll over in the bed to get some shut-eye. Tomorrow is going to be a long-ass day.

12

ANNIE

HOW DOES SOMEONE YOU BARELY KNOW FEEL LIKE THEY OWN YOUR SOUL?

I lie there holding my phone after Sabre's text. I can't sleep. I may have only been with him for a short amount of time, but I'm used to the way he spoons me and wraps his arms around me at night. He always takes one hand and wraps it around my breast, kisses my neck, and whispers goodnight in my ear. I've become addicted to that and have found that even one night without it and I'm wide awake. I crave him like an addict craves his next fix. I even want to cry after his text. That's how far I'm gone. I get up out of bed and walk to the bathroom, it's almost morning, I might as well stop pretending I'm going to sleep. The hour nap I had will be it.

After a quick shower, I stumble into the kitchen to find coffee. It's going to take a lot of coffee to get through today. It's just finishing up when there's a knock on my door. That single-girl-all-alone-it's-3 a.m. panic hits me. I walk cautiously to the front door, afraid it's Carl. He came by earlier today, said he heard talk I was living with a man. There was no sign of Sabre though and his old truck was hid in the garage, so I think I covered. Still, I know there is trouble coming on that front and I have no idea what I'm going to do about it. I go quietly to the door and glance through the peephole. Latch is standing on the other side. He's the man that Sabre has watching over me while he's out of town. He seems like a nice guy.

"What's up?" I ask, opening the door. I'm worried something happened since it's the middle of the night and he's here.

"I was wondering if my sister could spend what's the rest of the night here. She got picked up at a local party and the deputy called me to come get her. I can't trust her not to go back out if I'm not there." He pulls a sullen-looking young girl from the side of the house; I hadn't noticed her before. She's beautiful. Her hair is the color of midnight and she's got these deep, inky dark eyes and long, thick eyelashes. Her skin is pale and flawless, and she could easily be on the cover of any magazine, coming or going. She's also full of anger and looks like she wants to kill someone.

"Sure, come on inside," I tell them both, opening the door wider and stepping back.

"Annie this is my baby sister, Lucy. Lucy, this is Annie, she's Sabre's old lady."

"I'll be seventeen in two weeks, I'm not a baby," she grumbles.

"I think we're always babies to our big brothers. I know I was," I tell her trying to make her feel better as I lead them into the kitchen.

"Was? How on Earth did you get him to stop treating you like a child?" Lucy asks.

"Well, my brother died in a car accident and there's not been a day since then I haven't wished he was back here to be over-protective again," I answer, hoping my message gets across. I watch out of the corner of my eye and see her look at Latch.

"I just made a pot of coffee, would you guys like some?"

"Thanks, that sounds great. I didn't want to bother you, but I saw you had your light on and figured it'd be better for Lucy to sleep here instead of my truck."

"Why on Earth are you sleeping in your truck?"

"Remember, Sabre asked me to keep an eye on you. I can't hardly do that Annie if I'm not around."

"I thought you went home! You can't stay outside all night. I'll fix you a bed on the couch, and Lucy can have my spare room."

"Annie, we should probably talk about that with Sabre, and I don't mind...."

"Just hush it, I'll go find some clean sheets. Lucy, if you want to follow me, I'll show you where your room will be, sweetheart. You can get settled and then come out and have some coffee, or I could warm you some milk."

"Warm milk? Please. That sounds so gross."

I laugh, "It kind of does, but it actually helps relax you. I was just about to make me some. Sabre texted me to let me know they made it okay, and I was just too keyed up to go back to sleep."

"So they're all good?" She asks and she seems interested, maybe just a little *too* interested.

"Yes, I believe so. You know how they are. They never give too much information."

"Yeah, I do. I know them all though Latch doesn't let me hang around at the clubhouse much anymore."

"Really, why's that?" I ask, opening the door to the room she'll be staying in.

"He says I'm too old. One of the guys started asking me out and shit. I thought Latch was going to pop his lid. He doesn't seem to get that I'm not a little kid anymore."

"I get that, but he's your brother. Still, you are just sixteen so that's a little young for one of the members to be wanting to take you out on a date."

"It was Keys. He's only six years older than me, but it's not him I'm interested in," she says plopping down on the bed.

"So, there is someone in the club you are interested in?"

"Yeah, but it doesn't matter. He doesn't see me as anything other than a child and he'd never stand up to Latch to ask me out, even if he did."

"Well, you're too young to think about settling down anyway. But if it's meant to be, when the time is right, it'll happen. Look at me. I'm twenty-six and had given up the idea of ever finding someone I could love, and then my car broke down and I found Sabre."

"Yeah, maybe, thanks for the room, Annie. I wasn't doing anything wrong at the party, but I guess some of the neighbors thought we were too loud and called the law."

"It's okay. You get settled and come on out when you're ready. I'm just going to get some sheets and things for you brother and get him settled on the couch."

I spend the next hour or so talking with Latch and his little sister. I really like her. She's sweet, funny, and a really good kid. I get the feeling she's hanging with the wrong crowd and that's why Latch is concerned. I also get a bigger feeling that she's got a huge crush on Beast. That's bad news. He's a good sixteen or seventeen years older than her and there's no way he'll ever see her as more than a little girl, even after she becomes legal. Hopefully, that will work itself out. Once I get them settled, I head back to mine and Sabre's room. I reach over and grab Sabre's pillow and pull it into my body, hugging it tightly. I can smell his aftershave on it, and I inhale deeply. Just the scent alone is enough to relax me, and I feel my eyes closing fast. My last thoughts are that of Sabre. *I really do love him.*

13

SABRE

It feels as if I've been gone for a month, rather than just three days. I have a lot on my plate in the upcoming days with the club. I'm not the club enforcer or the Vice President, but as record keeper of the club and one of the main officers, I have a lot on my plate as we figure out where to go after our meeting with the Donahue brothers. Still, I've already told Skull and Pistol that I'm doing jack shit until I get the night with my woman.

With that in mind, as the other men turned into the club, I kept going and drove like a bat out of hell to get home. The minute I pull into the driveway and see Annie's old beat up vehicle I feel a sense of peace. I'm barely off my bike when Annie comes running out. She jumps straight into my arms and I have to plant my feet to keep from being bowled over by her. She's laughing and her eyes are alive with happiness. Her arms go around me and mine lock around her and that feeling of peace only intensifies.

"I missed you, Sabre. I'm so glad you're home."

Home. Yeah, I am definitely home.

"I missed you too, sweet Annie, and I'm getting ready to show you just how much," I growl picking her up in my arms and marching up the steps into the house. She is nibbling on my neck and telling me how much she's glad I'm home, and I wish I could hear her better. The truth is there's blood roaring in my ears, my cock is rock hard, and I have to have her. I feel like a damn monk who is about to break a seven-year vow of celibacy. I open the door, Annie still in my arms and freeze. Latch is sitting at the bar, eating. My eyes narrow in on him.

"What the fuck are you doing here?" I bark, my dick somehow growing harder.

"Having dinner. You just missed Lucy. She had dance practice."

I set Annie down with a sigh. No way. I am not going to get cock-blocked again and Annie is not ready for playtime.

"Annie. Bedroom, now. Take your clothes off and get on the bed and wait for me."

"Sabre."

"Now, Annie."

"Remind me again why I like the things you do to me," she grumbles leaving the room.

"I'm about to remind you. Latch, get the fuck out of here," I growl, my patience gone.

"Bye, Latch. Don't forget, you and Lucy are having dinner here Thursday night," Annie calls out.

"Wouldn't miss it, Peaches," Latch says with a wicked grin.

"I see you've made yourself at home," I say watching him closely. He's got that look in his eye that I haven't seen in a long time. My Annie has caught him, I knew she would. Hell, I just had to see her from a distance.

"She's special," he answers.

"She is."

"She doesn't let you keep your distance," he answers and I

nod my head in agreement. "Do I report to the club or here tomorrow?"

"Here, I'm going to be busy at the club for the next few days."

"You got it. Be good to her, brother," he says, slamming the door shut. I sigh. There are things to discuss with Latch, but I need Annie, it will have to happen later.

I go straight to the bedroom and what I find there takes my breath away. Annie is on the bed, gloriously naked, except for the sheet she has pulled over her. I should have told her I didn't want her covered up. I know she's shy. I know she's never done this before. A better man would understand that and move forward carefully. That is not who I am though, and Annie knows that. It'd be wrong for me to be any way other than the way I always plan to be with her.

"Come over here and undress me, Annie."

Her cheeks darken in color, but she slides out of bed and comes to me. She's beautiful as always, but knowing what we're about to do and what she is about to give me makes her even more so. She comes to a stop in front of me.

I can't stop my hand from coming up and caressing her collarbone and following the delicate path to her neck. "So beautiful."

Her hand gently covers mine and her sweet voice feels as if it takes ten years of darkness away from me.

"That's how I feel every time I look at you, Sabre."

So sweet, she could make my teeth ache. Her innocence intrigues me, but I can't wait to show her how good being bad can be. I take off my cut and toss it to the chair across from us, and then pull my shirt off. Her hands move over my stomach, her fingers moving slowly as if she's memorizing every line. Bit by bit she moves up my chest, her hands breaking apart and each thumb searching out my hard, small nipples and petting them. The touch is erotic and innocent at the same time.

I've done my best to bring Annie to this point; knowing what to expect from me. Each time I touched her brought her to orgasm; in the way I talked to her, texted, and in the videos or other things I made sure she watched. I'm not a tender man, not by a long shot. Annie brings out instincts and feelings I've never had before. Yet, sex is elemental to who I am. She may start off a virgin, but I plan to show her every forbidden pleasure my mind can dream up and make her want it...need it...*crave it*.

"I thought you told me to undress you?" she asks, placing a gentle kiss on my chest.

"I left the best parts for you," I grin.

"I'm a little nervous," she admits and I can hear her voice tremble.

I bring her face up close to mine, taking in all the myriad of emotions her eyes are trying to show and then kiss her softly. Our lips caress and graze each other in a slow dance that is intended only to divert her and to amp up her excitement.

I use my teeth to pull her lower lip into my mouth, sucking on it. I nibble it, let my tongue taste its flavor, all the while letting my hands pet and follow the contours of her body. I can't resist massaging those sweet, luscious globes and bringing her even closer to me. I could be wrong, but I think that's what pushes her over the edge and to the point her nerves take a back seat because she practically takes over our kiss. Her tongue forges into my mouth, trying to own it. Her hands move down to my sides and her fingernails bite into the skin, and the sweet sting of pain mixed with need acts like a drug in my system. I wanted to take this slow and easy the first time. Being with Annie doesn't allow that, I just can't. Together the two of us always end up being a raging wildfire.

"Annie...I can't be slow. You deserve someone who can take his time and worship you patiently. Fuck, sweetheart. I don't have it in me," I tell her when we break apart. My voice is unsteady from the need coursing through my veins.

"I don't want you to be anything other than the man I fell in love with." The words lie there for a second and they're backed up by the trust shining in her eyes. I may not be soft or able to give her what she deserves, but I vow I will make this good for her. I just hope I can. I know nothing about virgins. My darker desires always made me run from them.

"You can undress me next time...get up on the bed, now, Annie," I order. She backs away and when the bed presses against her legs, slides upon it. Her eyes stay on me the entire time. I like that, I will demand it from her—especially when I introduce her to the pleasures of having more than just me and her in our play-time. I bank those thoughts down as an image of Latch touching my woman tries to plant itself in my mind. It will happen, but tonight belongs to Annie and me.

I undress, letting her watch it all. My hand strokes up and down my cock, my pre-cum already making it slick and wet. I lie down beside her, nibbling on the side of her neck. I make small bruises there. I know she likes it, and I need to mark her every-where. I kiss a path down her chest, sucking on the pebbled nipple while my fingers play with the other. She gasps and her back comes off the bed from the sensation. Her hands wrap around my head pulling me harder against her. *Delicious.*

I let my hand drift to her sweet spot. She's soaked. I fight back the urge to thrust inside of her. Instead, I let my fingers play. I start gently, massaging them back and forth in the slick, sweet excitement that's gathered. I prime her clit, a combination of pushing and pulling that I know will get her where I need her to be. I'm dying to taste her again, but my dick will revolt at this point, not to mention my poor balls.

"Sabre..."

Her voice is vibrating with need. Her body thrusting and clenching my fingers, already. The fact that she can get this excited, this easily—is a gift. I kiss my way back to her neck, posi-tioning myself over her.

"You're so beautiful, Annie," her eyes open slowly, so crystal blue and clear. She looks at me with all the trust in the world. I slide two fingers inside her pussy. Over the brief time we've been together I've been slowly stretching her, waiting for this day, but there's only so much you can do with your hands. It's almost a struggle to sink two fingers into her. Her muscles tighten instantly and she tries to ride them. I hold them still inside her, using my thumb to continue manipulating her clit. "So beautiful and all mine."

"Sabre," she gasps out as I begin to fuck her in earnest with my fingers, bringing her body quickly to the point of orgasm. I should be ashamed for not going slower, for not giving her the sweet, slow seduction she should have. She deserves all of that and more, but the truth is I'm going to go crazy if I don't get inside of her.

I kiss along her darkened pink breast, sucking on the hardened nipple again and just as I feel her pussy spasm around my fingers, I bite down and pull with my teeth. My woman likes a little pain; I'm going to teach her to crave it. She has no idea just what her body is going to be searching for. The thought of being the one to give it to her is a rush like no other I've ever had in my life.

As she tumbles into her orgasm, her body shaking and calling out my name, I position my cock at her entrance. I watch as it all overtakes her. It's a familiar sight. I never let a day go by that I haven't given this to her, and usually much more than once a day, but somehow each time it just gets better.

"Annie," I groan, my cock literally leaking to get inside of her and it takes all of the control that I've mastered over the years to keep from thrusting home. Her nails are biting into my back and her body is pushing up into my hand, riding it and taking every ounce of pleasure she can find. It's beautiful, true, but I need her eyes. "Annie!" Her eyes snap to mine, hers are hazy and cloudy with pleasure. She's flushed, her lips swollen and wet and my cock slides forward just so the tip sits inside of her—resting...waiting.

"Sabre..."

"Keep your eyes on me, Annie. This is going to hurt, but I promise you it will get better."

"Please, Sabre. I want you," she answers, even as her head goes back and another wave hits her.

My mouth crashes down against hers as I drink in her taste and swallow her cries. My cock slides deeper inside. It feels like a damn vise gripping my cock and squeezing it. I feel the thin wall that keeps me from sinking further. This is important. I will be Annie's first man. Her first everything. I will fucking be her last, but then she will get that from me, too. I know I will never want another woman but Annie. *Ever.* With that thought ringing in my brain, I break away from her sweet lips. My mouth finds that soft juncture where her neck and shoulder meets, and I bite down and force my hard cock inside her body. She cries out, and I still. Her head is pressed into her pillow. The heels of her feet are shoved deep into the mattress and I'm balls deep inside of this beautiful creature—afraid to move.

Slowly, her eyes open and she looks at me.

"I'm yours now," she whispers. My heart beats hard against my chest.

"You've always been mine, Annie. Since the day you were born. You were made for me," I tell her starting my ride. She mews this sweet little sound and finds my rhythm and meets me thrust for thrust. My balls tighten and I feel the tingling zip down my spine; I'm about to come harder than I ever have in my life. Before I do, there's one thing I need to do—one thing I need to give her.

"I love you, Annie. I love you. This seals it, sweetheart. You're never getting away from me."

"Love for a lifetime?" she asks, her nails moving down to my ass as she pulls at me, trying to get me deeper. Hell, my balls are pressed against her hot pussy now and wet with her sweet liquid.

"For several, Annie...for fucking *ever*," I groan, riding her hard and losing myself in my own climax even as I feel her second one overtaking her, as my cum shoots inside of her. She clinches me so fucking tight, my eyes roll back in my head.

She's everything...*everything.*

14

ANNIE

JUST WHEN YOU THINK LIFE IS PERFECT, YOU FIND
YOURSELF STANDING IN FRONT OF A RATTLESNAKE AND NO
WEAPON AT HAND.

I've officially been Sabre's old lady for a month now and each day just gets better, and I'm not talking just sex—that is phenomenal, however. We make love constantly. Sabre is insatiable. It doesn't matter where we're at; he's made love to me in the bathrooms at the local department store even. He doesn't try to hold himself back, and I don't want him to. He makes me feel desirable, sexy, and like I'm the only woman in the world who can satisfy him. I may have been a virgin at twenty-six, but I'm pretty sure that I've had more sex than any woman on the face of the Earth. In fact, life is so perfect I've almost forgotten about the one thing that could ruin it all for me. That was a mistake. I know that from the number that just showed up on my caller ID.

Sabre is at the club, he's been dealing with some stuff; I'm not sure what, I don't ask. I figure if Sabre wants me to know anything about the club he'll tell me. As long as he's safe, I'm okay. I'm doing laundry while Lucy is in the living room doing her home-work. Latch is in the kitchen fixing a leaking faucet. They've become part of the family and are nearly always here. I love it, and I get the feeling that Sabre enjoys it, too—it makes him happy. I care for Latch, obviously not like I do Sabre, but still, I love him. He's a good guy who has a lot on his plate. Sometimes I catch him looking at me and my stomach gets butterflies. Sabre says Latch is halfway in love with me, but it doesn't seem to upset him. I figure it's because he trusts both of us. He should, my heart belongs to him and always will.

The phone call stops all of my thoughts and happy feelings, though. I stare at the caller ID, wishing I could just ignore it.

"Hello, Uncle Carl." My voice is straining.

"Annie, I think it's time we had a talk."

"I'm sorry, I can't. I have a dinner party…"

"Find a way to make it happen. I'd hate to get your father involved. We both know what happens when you get out of hand."

My stomach clenches. I've tried to block that out of my mind over the years. I was twenty-four and fresh out of college when I went on a date to the local football game. Kent Darby was a math teacher who asked me out and I agreed. I had met him a few times at school functions and football games; however, I didn't know that he was married. If I had, I never would have agreed. We went out and after dinner, he took me to the local marina and parked. We started talking and it was a fun evening until he started touching me and pushing me to do more with him.

I was inexperienced because of my father, so I had pretty much steered away from men. That night was freeing; I liked it. It got intense; he ripped my shirt. I don't think he meant to do it; I wasn't exactly fighting him off, I was curious. But, my door was ripped open and my father drug me out. My breasts were hanging out because my shirt had lace at the top and I didn't wear a bra. When he saw me like that, *he lost it*. And when I say he lost it, I mean he went bonkers. He threw me to the ground and had two deacons from his church hold onto me. Then he went after Kent.

This is where Kent explained to my father that he was

married, and I had seduced him. *Lured him away by using sex. He was weak.* The words blurred after that, as well as their faces because I was crying. What woman wouldn't cry when she's being discussed like she is to blame for the fall of the human race. After ten minutes of discussing how women were to blame for the fall of man, Kent left. That's when my father began beating me. I passed out during the beating and woke up in my father's church. The water in the baptistery had been drained. I was in a chair in the middle of it, tied up, surrounded by my father and three of his most trusted deacons. I was anointed with oil and struck repeatedly by a belt they had blessed. The goal, ultimately, was to show the demon inside of me that they would not allow him to stay. They kept me tied up for three days. My clothes were ripped from my body and I was roughly washed by them to purify me. I honestly thought I might die. Then Sheriff Richardson found me, somehow. He showed up and convinced my father and his crazy henchmen to free me. With the stipulation they let me go to Kentucky, where my Uncle Carl lived, or he would arrest them and continue investigating.

The deal made me mad. I kind of hated the sheriff, even if he had saved me. He could have done more, but when it was all said and done, I was just glad to get away.

"Do you hear me, girl? You ignore me and I will make sure your daddy..."

"I hear you. When?" I ask, once his voice pulls me out of my thoughts.

"Tonight. Seven o'clock. I happen to know for a fact that man you live with has been staying out late at night. So you don't have an excuse. Meet me at the old Crossroads Church out on HWY 25. Get here and be alone, *or else.*"

He hangs up with that dire warning.

"What's up, Peaches?" Latch asks me as I hang up the phone. I'm sure something in my face alerts him to what I'm feeling.

"It's nothing," I lie, trying to shake it off. I turn to go back into the laundry room, a thousand different thoughts swarming in my brain.

I make it back there and my body starts shaking as realization fully sinks in. I forgot, from the time I've been in Kentucky, just how much I am afraid to be back around my father. Even when I thought about going back home, I never meant it. I never wanted that. My past has left me feeling so insecure and unworthy, and it took Sabre to show me that I am not only normal, but I am exactly what he wants. I'm who I need to be. I don't know what I believe about the next world, but I do believe that Sabre and I are meant to be together—that we are made for each other. I don't care if that does make me sound like a Pollyanna.

I stiffen when I feel arms come around me. For a split second, I think Sabre has come home, but it's Latch.

"What's wrong, Peaches? Talk to me, honey."

"That was my uncle. He wants to meet with me."

"Absolutely not. Sabre told me about your family. He'd shit a brick if he knew you even talked to one of the motherfuckers."

Even in my fear, I laugh at Latch's reply. "I need to meet with him, if I don't, he won't stop. It'd be best to attack this head on and try to avert disaster. If my father comes here, Sabre will kill him."

"Then the sorry bastard needs to be killed."

"Latch, I need to…"

"I'll call Sabre."

He doesn't give me a chance to reply before he has his phone out. *This won't go well.*

"Damn it!" Latch says, hanging up the phone.

"What's wrong?"

"Shaft says Sabre and the other members are at the old packing plant in a meeting; there's zero cell service out that way."

"It's okay, we can all talk tonight," I lie. I'm not going to tell him. I'm going to find a way to deal with this before my family takes my happiness from me. I can't let that happen. I do *not* want my father anywhere near the state of Kentucky.

I worry all evening about how I am going to get away from Latch. In the end, Lucy makes my job easy. She had forgotten her coach called a dance rehearsal, and Latch had to drive her to the school. By the time she tells him, he doesn't have time to get Keys to come out, and I somehow convince him I'll be fine. I give it five minutes after he leaves, get in my vehicle and drive out to the old church.

There is a car parked outside, and one lone light shines from the frosted green glass window. My hands are shaking and my heart pounding, but I do my best to tap my fear down and head inside. I open the door and look around. At first I don't see anything, and then from the darkened entryway to another room comes my worst nightmare. It isn't my uncle at all. It is my father. I turn to run back to my car, but I'm trapped by my uncle.

"Daughter, I hear you've taken up your old ways. *Jezebel.* Did I not warn you what would happen if you didn't repent your transgressions? All my hard work and you've let the demons overtake you once again. Don't worry, I know exactly how to save you from your transgressions."

15

SABRE

I ALWAYS AIM FOR MY ENEMIES' WEAKNESSES. I'M JUST NOT
USED TO HAVING MY OWN.

kull thought we should give Dragon's crew a heads up
about the Donahue Brothers, so for the past hour we've
been talking with the Savage Brothers. I barely make it
out of the plant's door before Latch's old truck comes zooming up
the parking lot. Only one thing would make him drive that way.
My heart stalls.

"Son of a bitch, Sabre. I told the damn woman to sit still. I was
only gone for thirty minutes," he starts.

"Where is Annie?"

"I don't know, man. I got back to the house and she was gone.
I had to take Lucy for her dance practice. It was thirty minutes,
tops!"

"Was there signs of a struggle? Any idea who might have
gotten her?" I ask, trying to fight through the panic. If anything
were to happen to Annie...

"I don't think anyone did, her car's gone. I think she left to
meet that fucking uncle. He called and she seemed real upset. I
tried to call you but cell signal is shit out here. Then Lucy had
practice. Fucking hell, I'm sure she went to meet him."

"Where at?" I ask already getting on my bike.

"That's just it, I don't know."

I holler at the rest of the club which are standing to the side talking to Dragon and Dancer, "Torch! My woman's in trouble. Check the GPS coordinates on that tracker you put in her car and call me. Like yesterday."

"On it!" He calls, already on his bike. The sound of pipes echoes in the air, as my brothers jump on their rides. I'm already on the road, though. Torch will call as soon as signal pops in so he can get the coordinates from his cell. I've got to keep my shit together long enough to save my woman. I don't know what the uncle has planned, but after hearing Annie tell me what her motherfucking father did to her before she fled to Kentucky, I figure it's not good.

It's about ten minutes, the single most torture-filled ten minutes I've ever endured before Torch finally calls me. I get the directions, push down the throttle, and pray nothing has happened to her.

I BARELY LET my bike come to a stop before I'm off of it. I'm running to the damn door and not giving one fuck about my back. I've got my club with me that can watch it, but I can deal with these miserable fucks on my own. I'll make them regret the day they were ever born.

What greets my eyes when I open the door is the last thing I expected. It will be something I tell my grandkids about, and I do plan on having grandkids. In fact, just seeing my woman right now makes me long to have children with her. Children that will be strong, sassy, and beautiful, just like their momma.

Annie is standing over her father screaming at him. I know it's him from the things she's yelling. He's unconscious, his eyes are swollen, red and wet. She's also hog-tied him with duct tape. She's giving him down the road and telling him what a sad fuck he truly is. Though not said in those words, the message is still there. The uncle isn't unconscious, but his eyes are also red, swollen and he's crying profusely. He's also been hog-tied.

"Annie, what the hell?" I ask flabbergasted that somehow my woman managed to stop two grown men from hurting her. I'm glad and I'm proud as hell. I'm just not sure I understand it all.

"I...Sabre?" She questions, stopping mid-tirade to answer me.

"What's going on here? How did you do this?"

"I'm not stupid, Sabre. I didn't show up here without my stun gun and mace. How did you find out where I was?"

"I never called you stupid, woman, but I'm starting to think I need to sleep with one eye open," I joke, my heart definitely feeling lighter now that I know she's okay.

"Very funny, Sabre."

"I try, now would you mind telling me what these two assholes were trying to do to you?" I ask, even though I have a good idea what.

"They seem to think I'm riddled with demons because I like sex with the man I love," She grumbles and uses the stun gun on her already unconscious father again.

My lips stretch into the biggest smile I believe I've ever had, even as I take the weapon from her hand. She looks up at me and it's then I see the tears in her eyes.

"I think I hate him," she whispers with tears in her eyes.

"I know baby, I know. I need you to go home with Latch while I see to a few things."

"I want you to take me home," she answers, the tears are trying to escape but she's doing her best to keep them contained.

"I'll be there baby, I just want to take out the trash."

"What are you going to do?"

"Show them what a real demon looks like."

"You won't kill them?" She asks and I study her face.

"You would care?"

"I hate them, and I know you said, sometimes, in your job you have to see to things I probably wouldn't like. But, if you kill them...I don't want you to even risk jail for the likes of them. They're not worth it. Plus...I know it sounds stupid, but he is my father."

"Then I won't kill them. I'll tell them an angel begged her demon for their lives. Now kiss me, woman."

"I love you, Sabre."

"Show me," I urge her and she gives me her lips. I've never been more proud of a woman in my life. She amazes me. I'm still going to tan her hide for risking her life, that's a given. We break apart slowly. The best thing I've ever done in my life is claim this woman.

"I'm going to tan your hide for scaring me, Annie."

She smiles through her tears and leans up on her tip toes to whisper next to my ear, "Well, at least something good came out of this then."

I laugh. I'm still mad at the fuckers who dared try to hurt my woman, but I laugh.

"Get your ass home, woman."

"Yes, Sabre."

"Practice those words, you'll need to know them tonight," I order her as she walks off, partly because everyone is listening.

She stops at the door, holds her head down for a second, and then shocks the hell out of me.

"I'll do my best to remember them, as long as the cookie monster comes out to play."

Every single brother in there starts laughing. Fuck me. After I get over the shock, I laugh, too. I laugh hard. Annie doesn't know it, but I honestly wasn't sure I could keep from killing her fucker of a father. She just saved his life. Still, Keys and Shaft will have to drag him and his sorry ass brother back to Illinois because they won't be walking for a little while. They'll also have a message to deliver to Annie's mom, personally. I watch as Latch and Annie leave the room and then turn to the boys. I look at Skull and he gives me the all good sign and nods his head in agreement. He knows where I'm coming from—no words are needed.

"Torch, you're in charge," I growl, taking off my cut and rolling up my sleeves."

"Of what?"

"Making sure I keep my promise to Annie and don't kill these weasels," I growl and grab her sorry uncle first. Hopefully, by the time I finish with him, her lousy excuse for a father will have come to.

"Don't we get to join, man? We all like Peaches," Shaft asks.

"No way. These motherfuckers are all mine," I tell him as I take off my belt. I think I'm going to start with a little eye for an eye. I'll just make sure their scars are much bigger than the ones Annie carries.

16

ANNIE

SOMETIMES BEING WICKED FEELS REALLY, REALLY GOOD.

W e make it back to the house about an hour later. Latch isn't really talking to me, and I know he's upset. I don't really know how to make that better, either. My brain is fried. I feel dirty for even having been in the same room with my uncle and father. I'm a little worried that Sabre lied and will kill them anyway. I shouldn't even care. It's kind of messed up that I do.

"Where's Lucy?" I ask to break the strained silence as I go to the fridge and get a bottled water for me and a beer for Latch.

"Staying over at a friend's house since I couldn't be there to pick her up in time," he growls, and when he does that he sounds almost like Sabre. I take him the beer that Sabre keeps in the fridge for him and the boys and hand it to him.

"I'm sorry, Latch, I didn't mean to cause you trouble."

He looks up at me with his dark eyes. His looks are so much like his sister's, except definitely more masculine and defined.

"You could have got yourself killed, Peaches. Do you know what that would have done to me?"

The words sound raw and full of emotion and my stomach

clenches. Sabre said Latch was in love with me. It makes me feel guilty. Sabre owns my heart, even if I am attracted to Latch.

"I'm sorry. I promise it won't happen again. I'm going to go take a bath before Sabre comes home."

"He won't be long, he's going to teach them a lesson and then have the boys take them back to Illinois," he says, still pouting and turning on the television.

I take that in. I'm glad. I meant what I said to Sabre. Surely, they'll be smart enough to leave me alone. I know, inside, it's over and I feel free.

An hour and a half later, I'm forced to get out of the tub because my skin is starting to wrinkle and prune. I spend extra time putting on the lotion that smells like sugar cookies that Sabre likes. Then blow dry and brush my hair out. Finally, I slip on Sabre's long T-shirt that says Devil's Blaze on it and falls down almost to my knees. I'm going to go straight to bed to wait on him. I can't deal with Latch pouting anymore or the conflicting emotions he gives me. When I walk out into the bedroom, I freeze. Sabre and Latch are both sitting in the chairs I keep in my reading corner.

"Sabre, I..."

"I told you not to do it, didn't I, Peaches?"

"But I just..."

"You just defied an order I gave you."

Sabre has always walked the edge of dominating me, and I love it. It speaks to something inside of me, but while I may appear meek to the outside world, I'm not, really. I don't want to spend my life with a man where he expects me to follow orders.

"I don't see why you're so upset, it was just..."

"Because you went against my orders. I told you to stay close to Latch and home until we figured out what to do about your uncle and things calmed down at the club. You agreed and then turned around and ignored it. That can't be allowed."

"Sabre, I'm not the type of girl who will obey a man. I mean, I'm not..."

"I believe I know that about you, Peaches. You give me hell constantly, woman, but when I give you an order, it is to keep you safe. My world is different than yours was. When you gave yourself to me, I made a damn vow that I would always protect you. Do you remember that?"

I swallow and nod my head in agreement. He did, and I loved it. Sabre makes me feel *special*. After a lifetime of feeling invisible, it's an amazing thing.

"Good, then you can understand why the fact that you defied my orders and went to the church tonight upsets me. Right?"

I feel a moment of shame because I do. He's right. I shouldn't have gone. Still, I know a moment of resentment and I have to defend myself.

"I had it under control. I'm sure you saw that when you got there. I didn't go empty-handed."

"They weren't expecting you to be the woman you are now. That was their mistake. This easily could have ended a lot different, and you wouldn't be able to stand there and continue to sass me. Now, say the words."

"I'm sorry, Sabre, I should have listened," I tell him looking down at my feet.

"Strip."

I gasp and look up at him in shock. He couldn't have said what I thought. *No way.*

"Strip," he confirms. I look around the room nervously. I can do this. Sabre's upset, obviously and with good reason. But he won't hurt me. In fact, I've liked all of the things he has done to my body. I've come to crave it.

"Peaches," he growls.

My eyes snap back to him. "I will! I was waiting for Latch to leave!"

"Latch isn't leaving, Peaches."

"Sabre, you can't...wait, what did you say?"

"You lied to Latch and he felt this was his fault. If you had gotten hurt, it would have haunted him. He deserves something for that. So, he's going to help punish you. Now, strip."

I look at Sabre then Latch and back to Sabre. I can't do this! *Can I?* My heart is tripping over itself. I wish I could run away. Still, underneath my panic, there's a big part of me wanting this. Wanting to see where this goes...and that scares me. Sabre has stormed into my life and let the tight leash I kept on my desires loose. This is a huge step in a direction I'm not sure I want.

"Annie, look at me." I do, and I know he can see the fear in my eyes. "You got your safe word. Nothing happens that you won't like, baby. I can promise you that."

I study his expression and know he's serious, and I also see that look on his face that spoke to me from day one. *Need.* That gives me the courage to lift the shirt over my head. I let it fall to the floor.

I keep my eyes on Sabre at all times. I may be attracted to Latch, but Sabre needs to know he's the one in control here. *I need him to know that.*

"Go sit in Latch's lap," Sabre orders, his voice dark and gruff, and it feels like a caress on my skin, grating each tiny nerve cell I possess.

I do as he asks and wait. I'm not sure what Sabre has in mind here, but I know wherever it leads, he will take care of me. Latch's jeans are rough against my skin, and I jump when his large hands stroke down my sides and squeeze my hips gently. He's breathing rough, but then so am I. My eyes are locked on Sabre. He's unzipped his pants and has his cock in his hand, stroking the hard, glistening member and instantly, my mouth waters. I'm so engrossed with watching Sabre that I wasn't expecting Latch's hands to come up and hold my breasts. I jump at the sensation. He kneads them, placing a kiss on my shoulder. Excitement floods my system and I'm so wet, I can feel the moisture on the inside of my thighs.

"Are you wet for us, Peaches? Is your clit throbbing, needing attention?" Sabre asks and I search his eyes, but I can't find any disappointment there.

I give him the truth and nod my head yes.

"The words, Peaches. Give me the words."

It doesn't escape my attention that he's calling me Peaches. He said Annie was his and his alone. I don't know why that distinction calms me, but it does just the same.

"I'm wet, I'm so wet, Sabre."

"Check and make sure she's not lying Latch," he orders, his hand moving slow and steady up his cock. I can see a drop of liquid gather on the head and run down the side of his shaft onto his hand and I lick my lips, wishing I could taste it. I feel Latch's hand come between my legs, his finger dragging through my arousal. It's hot being in his arms and watching Sabre stroke himself, but it's not what I want.

"She's soaking wet, Sabre." Latch groans.

"Do you want my cock, Peaches?"

"God, yes," I answer, not even bothering to hide how eager I am. It's too late for that.

"Come over here and get down on your knees, Peaches, and I'll let you suck my cock."

I should be ashamed at how eagerly I jump off of Latch's lap. I get down on my knees so quickly, I'm surprised I don't have rug burns.

"So eager," he says cupping my cheek and pulling me to him as he bends down to kiss me. There's so much emotion in that kiss, more than I've ever felt before. "Do you get how much I care about you, Annie? How much it would kill me if something happened to you?"

His words hit me and tear me open inside. The change of the name doesn't get past me, and there's a depth of emotion coming from him that hasn't been there before, or at least where it was so evident. His eyes are intense and they speak of something... deeper. Of fear and caring certainly, but there's something else, I want to call it a sadness, a regret. I'm just not sure, and I'm way too aroused to study it further.

"I'm sorry Sabre, I won't do anything like that again. I'll always talk to you first."

His thumb brushes the corner of my lip, gently, and for a minute he looks so deep in thought it almost scares me. I want to ask him what's wrong, I can even feel the beginnings of panic flood through me. Then, this mask comes over his face. The change in him is that drastic, almost night and day.

"Now, Latch." His gruff, husky command rings in the room.

My body stiffens in response. I had forgotten all about Latch being in the room. I try to look behind me, but Sabre doesn't let me.

"Keep your eyes on me, Peaches. Always on me." I give him my nod of agreement and he combs his fingers through my hair. "Suck me, Peaches."

At his words, the tight coil of need inside of me breaks free. Sabre's holding his cock towards my mouth and I open for him, without a moment of hesitation. His warm, spicy, unique flavor fills my mouth and I moan with the pleasure. I release him and flatten my tongue out using it to lick along the hardened vein that is throbbing. I lick all the way to the top and then dive into the crevice on his head, gaining more of his pre-cum and savoring it. I repeat the action but along the side of his cock this time; licking him as if he were my favorite ice cream cone and I'm trying to get every drop before it melts. I'm so intent on Sabre that I didn't notice Latch get behind me. I feel his rough hands rub my ass and knead it in his strong hands. The effect is almost too much. I look up at Sabre and his eyes are all on me. I suck him down to the root as my excitement amps up. Latch's fingers brush the lips of my pussy. The very tips of his fingers slide between them and graze my opening. I widen my knees to offer him better access like a mindless animal in heat. I am. God, I'm so hot right now and dying to be filled. I never imagined sex could be like this. Elemental, hot, and all lust...this is fucking. This is totally different from anything Sabre and I do together and maybe that's good. Because, it should be different with Latch involved.

Latch's fingers slide into me at the same exact time Sabre's fingers tease one of my nipples. He rolls it between his finger and thumb, pulling on it until that moment where there's pain, but it's oh so good. Latch is slowly fucking me with his fingers and I thrust against it, tightening my pussy against the entry, trying to hold them inside. I'm so absorbed in the sensations bombarding at me, that when the first hard slap against my ass connects, I cry out loud. My scream comes out garbled because my mouth is full of Sabre. I slowly release him and look into his eyes as Latch spanks me again, and again. Each slap is hard, and I can feel the fiery heat against my skin. My eyes sting from the intense pain, and I'm waiting for that point. That point where the pain slowly morphs into pleasure. Sabre is watching me closely, stroking his cock the entire time. That's even hotter than what Latch is doing to me. Eventually, though, I feel it; that moment when I need more of a sting, more of what Latch is giving me. My cream is sliding down my legs. I'm thrusting up, seeking more contact and riding nothing but air; still needing more. I whimper as Sabre grabs my hair and pushes my mouth down on his cock. He resumes playing with my breast and over the rushing blood in my ears I hear his command.

"Now, Latch. You can taste her."

The intense way he says it is almost enough to set me off. I'm caught up in the different pleasures zooming through my body that I'm unprepared when I feel Latch's mouth against my pussy. Sabre stands up, taking his cock from me, but I don't have time to protest because he pushes me away from him, until I'm sitting up, straddling Latch's head.

"Ride him, Peaches. Fuck his face and ride him hard and take your pleasure," Sabre urges me—right before taking my hair roughly in his hands and pulling my mouth to his cock again. I grind against Latch's so hard, I'm probably smothering him. Rotating my hips, riding his tongue and hell, I think even his nose. Latch's hands push into my ass cheeks which are still stinging, and he lets his fingers bite into them, adding to my need. Then he takes control of my movements, angling them just enough to make me feel like I'm about to explode. I brace myself on Sabre's thighs, letting my hands hold him tightly as he continues fucking my mouth while I'm riding Latch.

Eventually, Sabre pulls me off of his cock and I look at him through eyes that are hazy with lust. I'm so near to coming, just another second and I know I'll tumble over the edge.

"Are you close, Peaches?"

"God, yes," I groan as Latch's tongue lashes against my clit. I try to bear down on his face. He uses his hold on me so that doesn't happen. I grunt out in defeat. "Are you frustrated, sweetheart? Does that greedy little cunt need to come because you've got two men in here dying to fuck you?" He asks and I can't stop a growl that breaks free.

"Sabre let me come, damn it. Let me come," I huff. My head tips back in pleasure as Latch continues to tongue fuck me and eat out my pussy but never giving me enough or in the right spot to carry me over the edge.

"Are you sorry for making us worry now, Peaches? Do you see why it's important to let me know what you're doing? How much you're loved and wanted?"

Tears sting my eyes, and it's not just because of being denied my pleasure. It's the words. *Loved and wanted.* I am. For the first time in my life, I am—and by two amazing men. I've always known Latch felt that way, but I've tried to hide from it because I can't give him what he needs. I was afraid to dream that Sabre felt that way. So the tears fall, and I let them.

"I'm sorry, Sabre. I promise never to worry you, either of you again like that. Please, sweetheart."

He growls and pulls me off of Latch, and I cry in protest. *I was so close.* I'm on the edge and ready to break into a million pieces. I just need one touch. One touch will send me over. I reach down to do it myself, but I don't get the chance.

"It's my pussy now, Peaches. *All mine.* I'll tell it when to come, I'll tell it how to come. You gave it to me. Remember?" Sabre questions.

"Yes!" I cry out, thinking his punishment may kill me.

He turns me around, yet again, my back to his front. The warmth of his body envelopes me as we slowly slide to the floor. He kisses on my shoulder, bites on the tender skin of my neck and follows an invisible trail up to my ear. His hands wrap in my hair again, harder this time, more intense. He pulls it back and his breath is against my ear.

"You are mine. Every fucking, single inch of you is mine. Do not ever get that shit confused, Annie."

"I won't...I couldn't." I tell him, gasping as his hands cup my soaked pussy.

"You be a good little girl and suck Latch's cock and make him come. You owe him that. So, I'm giving him that. Not you, *me.* You see the difference, Annie."

"Yes..." I do, absolutely. I'd never do this without Sabre wanting it and directing it.

"This thing with Latch is special, Annie. So he gets to have the parts of you I'm willing to give him. You're going to give it to him good. You're going to suck him down like the greedy girl you are. But you gave me your pussy. I will be the one who decides when it gets cock. I will be the one to decide when it comes, how it comes and by whom. It's mine. Understand?

"God, yes," I groan.

"Good. Now suck off Latch and I'll give your pussy what it needs."

I go back to my hands and knees once Sabre releases my hair. He leans over me, even in my haze I can feel him there. He places a tender kiss against my lower back.

LATCH HAS MOVED SO he's standing and holding his cock out for me. There's emotion shining in his eyes that I don't fully understand. I cup his balls in my hand first, rolling them with my fingers and then slide my tongue against them, using my hand to stroke his cock at the same time. I suck one ball in my mouth, gently torturing it before releasing and doing the other. Then I move to his cock, licking my way up to the tip. He's different. The taste, the smell, texture...it's all different from Sabre. It's good, and I take a moment to savor and take the pleasure in before I swallow him down all the way to the root. He's not as long as Sabre, so it's easier. He is wide though, so he still stretches my mouth. I suck him hard, moving up and down on his cock and using my hand at the same time. I get so engrossed in what I'm doing that when Sabre slides his cock inside of me, I'm taken by surprise. I finish my downward thrust of Latch's cock and rest there. My mouth and throat is stretched with Latch's dick, my pussy stretched with Sabre's and I'm loving every minute of it.Then Sabre starts moving and my desire hasn't even come close to waning. Immediately, I feel my climax building. I quicken my movements, sucking him harder, using my tongue to bathe, torture, and tease with every stroke, my hand working him harder, up and down, so that I can use my throat and let him go deeper every time Sabre thrusts inside of me.

We work together in some kind of three part dance that fits together perfectly because in no time, I'm coming. I come harder than I ever have before. I can feel my release rushing over Sabre's cock deep inside of me. I stumble in the way I'm working Latch's cock and he takes over. He puts both hands on my head and force feeds me his cock. There's nothing sweet and loving about it. It's hot, nasty, and so fucking good I barely finish coming before I shoot off again like a rocket. This one is more intense, and I lose track of everything except wave after wave of pleasure that pounds me. I feel Sabre's cum jetting inside of me, each stream feeling as if it is a thrust itself. He's seated so deep inside of me I know I'll be wickedly sore tomorrow, and I'll love every minute of it. Latch groans above me and I open my eyes and watch as complete satisfaction comes across his face. I get just a small taste of him before he pulls out of my mouth and finishes coming in his hand. I watch as the creamy pearl liquid runs down his hand and over his cock, and the sight of it along with the way Sabre's fingers start working my clit send me over into another climax. This one is so huge, so fucking explosive, it scares me. I try to fight it off, but Sabre's voice is in my ear, talking me through it, and I let him anchor me and give myself over to the orgasm, welcoming it.

I think I black out for a minute, I'm not quite sure. When I open my eyes, Latch has cleaned up and his pants are zipped. I'm sitting on the floor in Sabre's arms. Latch moves his fingers along my lips and has a melancholy smile that hurts me just a little.

"You're a special woman, Peaches," he says kissing my head gently then leaves the room.

I watch him go with more than a little sadness. Sabre kisses the top of my head and hugs me a little tighter, and I concentrate on him and my love for him.

17

SABRE

I NEVER THOUGHT I'D BE COMPLETELY OWNED BY A
WOMAN. I AM. I'M SO FUCKING GONE OVER THIS WOMAN,
THERE'S NO COMING BACK FROM IT.

I take Annie into our bath to wash off. We have a quick shower; she's almost boneless from our workout so I bring her to our bed. Our little playtime was hotter than hell, but I am a possessive motherfucker. There's no other man getting in Annie's bed but me. I pull the sheet over us, hold her close, and think there's nowhere on Earth that I'd rather be.

"Is Latch going to be okay?" she asks and I knew she'd see it. My brother has had it bad for her, almost as long as I have. Latch and I are super close. We're connected in ways that no one but the two of us knows, or will ever know. Tonight was my gift to him, but I'm a big enough bastard to admit, it was a gift to me, too. I fucking loved watching Annie be overcome and get so fucking hot, not just for me—but both of us. I loved watching every minute of her pleasure and Latch's. It's bigger than that, though. I liked being the one in complete control of both of their pleasures.

"He'll be fine, sweetheart. He knows the score. We'll be playing again, sometime. As long as you liked it?"

She's quiet for a minute and I'm afraid she's gone too far. She enjoyed it, but I don't want it to be something she can't live with.

That's the reason I gave her a safe word. Anything we do, I need both of us to be in it a hundred percent.

"Annie?"

"I did, but..."

"But?" I ask, knowing fear because I want this again. Not often, but I do want it. I was hoping she'd feel the same.

"It sounds awful, Sabre."

"Tell me, sweetheart. Never be afraid to tell me anything."

"I loved it. It was hot and even now I could see wanting it again, but..."

"But, what?"

"It would kill me if you were with another woman. I couldn't take it. I think it would destroy me. Now that we have done this, I mean you'd be in your rights, but I just couldn't...Oh, God..."

"Shhh...Sweetheart, don't get yourself so worked up," I tell her bringing her head at an angle so she can see me. I use the pads of my thumb to wipe away the tears. "Annie, I love you. You own me, woman. I will never want another woman in my life, but you. *Only* you."

"But, what we did here..."

"Happened because all three of us wanted it. You didn't cheat on me, Annie. We had hot fucking sex with a close friend. Someone we both care about. There's nothing wrong in that, there's no shame in it, and it's not a sign that we don't belong to each other."

"You're sure?" She asks, searching my face.

"I'm completely sure. We're it, Annie. You and me woman are a lifetime thing. You know that, right?"

Her tears start again and I can't keep up to stop them, but she's smiling, so I figure it's okay.

"I love you, Sabre. I love you so much."

"Enough for a lifetime?" I ask.

"Enough for several," she answers and that's all the answer I need.

I lean over the side of the bed and reach under to the box I had stored there a few days ago. I've been waiting for the right time, and I don't think there can be a more perfect one than now.

I pull out the white box and she sits up like a little kid excited for Christmas.

"What's this?"

"Open it and see," I laugh as she claps her hands.

She rips into the box quickly, giggling madly and pushing the tissue paper inside away. All laughter stops though as she puts her hand on the leather cut inside. Her fingers graze over the Devil's Blaze emblem and then tremble as she takes in the white patch underneath.

Property of Sabre.

I wait for a response. It seems like forever.

"A lifetime worth of love," she whispers.

"Several," I correct her.

"Put it on me," she says, holding it up. I shake my head but do her bidding. She is on her knees leaning over me, naked as the day she was born, except for the leather Devil's Blaze cut and my dick goes hard as a rock. She's never been prettier. There has *never* been anything sexier in my life, than her. "I want you to make love to me now. Just like this. I want to have you inside of me while I'm wearing your colors. I need you to make love to me, Sabre.

I can do nothing but give her what she wants—what we both want.

EPILOGUE

SKULL

"You don't understand the devastation of words, until you see the damage and realize you can't take them back."

"I'VE MISSED YOU, querida. I need to feel you close to me."

"I'm here Skull. I'll never leave you."

"But you have mi amor. It's so dark here without you. I need your ligero. You kept me sane."

"You killed me, Skull. I can't ever be with you again. I'm visiting the only way I can. The only way they will allow me."

"Who are they? Who are these people who seek to keep my mujer from me. I will hunt them down. Nothing can keep us apart. Nada!"

"That's not true. Even now you are in bed with another woman."

"A club whore, nothing else," I dismiss.

"But she's not a whore, Skull. Not this one. This one cares

about you. This one you pursued. She has a place in your club. In your life. You're slowly forgetting me."

"Never!" I scream as she starts fading away. Querida, come back to me. No me dejes solo!"

"But you're not alone. You have her. You even took off my locket. I would have waited for you, Skull. I would have waited," she says, crying before she fades into the black. My body jerks from the pain on her face and I jar myself awake.

I rake my hand through my hair, despising the way it trembles. I move to the side of the bed, putting my feet on the floor. I'm hung over as hell. My head, my teeth and even my fucking hair hurts. I look at the blonde in my bed. I've been pursuing her since Dragon's so called funeral. She reminded me so much of Beth. The blonde hair, the unusual eyes. I saw her and went after her. In the end she was nothing like my Beth, but she's a good woman. A woman a man could claim. If he was whole. If he had every piece of him. If he wasn't haunted.

My cell phone rings and I grab it off the nightstand. Walking away from the bed. I'm not ready to talk to her...to anyone. My emotions are still raw. When I see who is on the phone, I know it's not going to get any better.

"You weren't at the meeting with your brother," I mutter, wishing I was completely done with all of the Donahues...with everything. I'm starting to hate Beth. Hate her for bringing this shit in my life and leaving me in it.

"I did not know about it. I am in France trying to calm the family. The death of my grandfather has left us all scrambling."

"Si, for power."

"True. But my grandfather was revered. They want his death avenged. Who killed the motherfucker. I'd like to buy him a beber, hell maybe four."

"I thought Colin told you?"

"What the fuck are you talking about?"

"Beth, she is alive. My grandfather was keeping her and her sister prisoner. They murdered him and fled."

"I don't know what kind of game you and your brother are playing, but I am not..."

"It is no game, Skull. It is very real. And the family has called a hit out on the girls. They have tracked them down in Texas."

My hand shakes. Is it? Could it be real? After my meeting with Colin, I started taking precautions, but I thought he was playing me. There was no way she could have survived...I look over at the woman in my bed, and something coils inside of me I do not want to name.

"What is your game Matthew?" I ask, because though he is slightly better to deal with than Colin, he's still a fucking Donahue and I do not trust him.

"There is a child, Skull. Your child."

"I saw Colin's papers. I know. I'm checking into it, but having some woman pretend to be Beth just so your family..."

"It is not pretend, Skull. Beth and your daughter are very much alive. At least until my family gets a hold of them."

There's so many things running through me right now, I couldn't name one fucking emotion except anger and bitterness....bitterness is overwhelming me. Could Beth have done this to me? Could she?

"What do you want with me? I know it's something."

"I called to see if you would work with us. If you will help us hunt down Beth and her sister. You bring them to me."

"What do I get out of this?"

"Revenge and something more valuable. You will have your daughter. If my family finds them first they won't care about the child. Some will take great pleasure in ending her young life."

"So. I just hunt down Beth and her sister, bring them to you and I keep mi hija, and that's it? That's all I have to worry about from you assholes? No more shit. We're done?"

"Exactly. Do we have a deal?"

I take a deep breath, and stare out into the night through the window.

"Sure. Give me the info and I'll get the men started on it."

"I must warn you if you double cross me, there will be consequences."

"There always are when the Donahues are involved. Give me the info. What part of Texas?"

Matthew rattles off the information and I write it down.

"Got it. I'll send the men out in the morning."

"I'm so glad we could work together again, Skull."

"Sure. Oh. One more thing, Matthew."

"What is that my friend?"

His words make me sick.

"Chinga te! The day I make any deal with a Donahue is the day I slit my own wrists."

I slam the phone down, shaking with anger and with the ramifications of what Matthew said. Where I was reluctant to believe what Colin said, I have very little doubt in Matthew's words.

"You okay mi amante?" Teena asks me from the bed. The news I just received, the dream of Beth it all combines, and a mixture of hate and guilt curls in my stomach. Adulterer. Beth has turned me into that. "Come back to bed. Let me make whatever it is better," she purrs.

I stand there wondering what in the fuck I'm going to do.

READ MORE JORDAN

Reading Order On Next Page

BOOKS DIVIDED BY SERIES

PLEASE NOTE SAVAGE BROTHERS AND DEVILS BLAZE MC
SERIES HAVE CHARACTERS THAT INTERACT WITH
EACH OTHER.

Doing Bad Things
Going Down Hard
In Too Deep

Savage Brothers MC
Breaking Dragon
Saving Dancer
Loving Nicole
Claiming Crusher
Trusting Bull
Needing Carrie

Devil's Blaze MC
Captured
Craved
Burned
Released
Shafted
Beast
Beauty

Lucas Brothers Series
Perfect Stroke
Raging Heart On
Happy Trail

Pen Name:
Baylee Rose
Filthy Florida Alphas Series
Unlawful Seizure
Unjustified Demands

LINKS:

Here's my social media links! Make sure you sign up for my newsletter. I give things away there and you get to see things before others! I also have a blog on my webpage you can subscribe to and besides my strange ramblings I'll update you on my work in progress and give you delicious secrets.... or boring ones!

Webpage Subscriber's Link:
https://www.jordanmarieromance.com/subscribe
Facebook Page:
https://www.facebook.com/JordanMarieAuthor
Twitter:
https://twitter.com/Author_JordanM
Webpage
http://jordanmarieromance.com
Instagram:
https://www.instagram.com/jordan_marie_author/
Pinterest:
https://www.pinterest.com/jordanmarieauth/

Bookbub:
https://www.bookbub.com/authors/jordan-marie

Made in the USA
Coppell, TX
26 October 2023

23389172R10066